Dear Reader,

The candles are on the cake and it's time for all of us to celebrate the 20th Anniversary of Silhouette Books. What an incredible number that is…twenty years!

You, the loyal readers, are the ones who should blow out the candles and be served the first pieces of cake. Without you, the authors who write these books and the editors who are partners with those authors would be only daydreaming about such a momentous event, instead of it being a reality.

I am very proud to be a part of the Silhouette family. Over the years there have been books that, hopefully, made you laugh, made you cry and caused you to sigh in contentment as you read the final page with its promise to you of a happy ending.

I want to personally thank each and every one of you for your continued support and for the lovely letters you've written to me to let me know that you enjoy my books. Those letters mean more to me than I can begin to tell you. Each one is answered by me, then tucked away in my treasure album.

As we look toward the next twenty years of Silhouette Books, I wish all of you good health, happiness and the fulfillment of your dreams.

With warmest regards,

Joan Elliott Pickart

Dear Reader,

Happy 20th Anniversary, Silhouette! And Happy Valentine's Day to all! There are so many ways to celebrate...starting with six spectacular novels this month from Special Edition.

Reader favorite Joan Elliott Pickart concludes Silhouette's exciting cross-line continuity ROYALLY WED with *Man...Mercenary... Monarch,* in which a beautiful woman challenges a long-lost prince to give up his loner ways.

In *Dr. Mom and the Millionaire,* Christine Flynn's latest contribution to the popular series PRESCRIPTION: MARRIAGE, a marriage-shy tycoon suddenly experiences a sizzling attraction—to his gorgeous doctor! And don't miss the next SO MANY BABIES—in *Who's That Baby?* by Diana Whitney, an infant girl is left on a Native American attorney's doorstep, and he turns to a lovely pediatrician for help....

Next is Lois Faye Dyer's riveting *Cattleman's Courtship,* in which a brooding, hard-hearted rancher is undeniably drawn to a chaste, sophisticated lady. And in Sharon De Vita's provocative family saga, THE BLACKWELL BROTHERS, tempers—and passions— flare when a handsome Apache man offers *The Marriage Basket* to a captivating city gal.

Finally, you'll be swept up in the drama of Trisha Alexander's *Falling for an Older Man,* another tale in the CALLAHANS & KIN series, when an unexpected night of passion leaves Sheila Callahan with a nine-month secret.

So, curl up with a Special Edition novel and celebrate this Valentine's Day with thoughts of love and happy dreams of forever!

Happy reading,

Karen Taylor Richman,
Senior Editor

Please address questions and book requests to:
Silhouette Reader Service
U.S.: 3010 Walden Ave., P.O. Box 1325, Buffalo, NY 14269
Canadian: P.O. Box 609, Fort Erie, Ont. L2A 5X3

JOAN ELLIOTT PICKART

MAN...MERCENARY...MONARCH

Silhouette®

SPECIAL ✦ EDITION®

Published by Silhouette Books
America's Publisher of Contemporary Romance

Special thanks and acknowledgment are given
to Joan Elliott Pickart for her contribution to
the Royally Wed series.

For Olive Elliott,
because it's time to pause and say,
"Thanks, Mom!"

 SILHOUETTE BOOKS

ISBN 0-373-24303-0

MAN...MERCENARY...MONARCH

Copyright © 2000 by Harlequin Books S.A.

This edition published by arrangement with Harlequin Books S.A.

® and TM are trademarks of Harlequin Books S.A., used under license.
Trademarks indicated with ® are registered in the United States Patent
and Trademark Office, the Canadian Trade Marks Office and in other
countries.

Visit us at www.romance.net

Printed in U.S.A.

Books by Joan Elliott Pickart

Previously published under the pseudonym Robin Elliott

JOAN ELLIOTT PICKART

is the author of over seventy novels. When she isn't writing, she enjoys watching football, knitting, reading, gardening and attending craft shows on the town square. Joan has three all-grown-up daughters and a fantastic little grandson. In September of 1995, Joan traveled to China to adopt her fourth daughter, Autumn. Joan and Autumn have settled into their cozy cottage in a charming small town in the high pine country of Arizona.

IT'S OUR 20th ANNIVERSARY!
We'll be celebrating all year,
continuing with these fabulous titles,
on sale in February 2000.

Special Edition

 #1303 Man...Mercenary... Monarch
Joan Elliott Pickart

 #1304 Dr. Mom and the Millionaire
Christine Flynn

 #1305 Who's That Baby?
Diana Whitney

#1306 Cattleman's Courtship
Lois Faye Dyer

 #1307 The Marriage Basket
Sharon De Vita

 #1308 Falling for an Older Man
Trisha Alexander

Intimate Moments

 #985 The Wildes of Wyoming—Chance
Ruth Langan

 #986 Wild Ways
Naomi Horton

 #987 Mistaken Identity
Merline Lovelace

#988 Family on the Run
Margaret Watson

#989 On Dangerous Ground
Maggie Price

#990 Catch Me If You Can
Nina Bruhns

Romance

VIRGIN BRIDES **#1426 Waiting for the Wedding**
Carla Cassidy

BREWSTER BABY BOOM **#1427 Bringing Up Babies**
Susan Meier

#1428 The Family Diamond
Moyra Tarling

The WEDDING AUCTION **#1429 Simon Says...Marry Me!**
Myrna Mackenzie

#1430 The Double Heart Ranch
Leanna Wilson

#1431 If the Ring Fits...
Melissa McClone

Desire

 #1273 A Bride for Jackson Powers
Dixie Browning

 #1274 Sheikh's Temptation
Alexandra Sellers

#1275 The Daddy Salute
Maureen Child

#1276 Husband for Keeps
Kate Little

#1277 The Magnificent M.D.
Carol Grace

#1278 Jesse Hawk: Brave Father
Sheri WhiteFeather

Chapter One

Jake's Saloon looked like a set from a low-budget Western movie.

John Colton stood just inside the door of the noisy, smoke-filled building and swept his gaze over the milling crowd.

Strange, he thought. Nothing had changed during the years since he'd been in this place. It was Friday night in Hope, Arizona, and the randy cowboys from the ranches in the area were out in force. They had payday money in their pockets, and women on their minds.

It even smelled the same, a mixture of smoke, beer, cheap aftershave and the pungent aroma of male sweat, cattle and horses.

He'd catch a whiff now and then of too much

perfume worn by the multitude of women in tight jeans, or short skirts, or whatever they hoped might entice the cowboys on the prowl.

It was all very tacky, but it was real earthy and honest, exactly what it appeared to be, and it suited his needs at the moment just fine.

John unbuttoned his suede, fleece-lined jacket, revealing a dark blue Western shirt with pearly snaps, then tugged his black Stetson low on his forehead.

He made his way forward, inching past the tangle of bodies at the bar to reach the area with cracked-leather booths and scarred wooden tables that edged a worn dance floor.

Garth Brooks was wailing from a brightly colored jukebox about having friends in low places, and a raised platform against a far wall stood ready for the band that would play loud, country-western music later that night.

John slid into a booth that was closer to the congested bar area than he would have preferred, but it was the last available free space he could find.

He shrugged out of his jacket and tossed it across the table to land on the other seat, a clear indication, he hoped, that he wasn't open to having company. Like the majority of men in the nightclub, he left his Stetson firmly settled on his head.

He leaned back against the stiff leather and sighed deeply.

This was a crazy place to be, he supposed, considering he had some very serious thinking to do. But the walls of his room in the shabby-but-clean motel had been closing in on him, resulting in him pacing like a caged animal.

His jet lag, combined with the shocking, nearly unbelievable news he'd received, had sent his brain into overload, his thoughts chasing in an endless circle in his mind.

Man, oh, man, what was he going to do?

That question was hammering at him unmercifully. He had to have a plan, an answer, by tomorrow, for Pete's sake.

"Ah, hell," he said aloud, dragging both hands down his face.

"Rough goin', cowboy?" a female voice said.

John snapped his head around to see a waitress standing next to the booth, a pad of paper in one hand, a pencil in the other. She was wearing a very short red skirt with white fringe, a matching bolero top that exposed her midriff, and white cowboy boots. A white Stetson was cocked at a jaunty angle on her head.

"Yeah," John said, "you could say that."

"Well, you came to the right place," she said. "Some drinkin' and dancin' will take your mind off your troubles. What can I get ya?"

"Beer," John said.

"What kind?"

"Doesn't matter," he said. "I don't care. Bring me whatever is handy."

"Whew. You *are* bummed, big time. Hey, a good-lookin' guy like you can have your pick of any gal in the place. Get yourself a pretty woman and go for it. Be right back with your beer. You runnin' a tab?''

''Yeah.''

The waitress hurried away, managing to wiggle her hips despite her fast pace.

Get myself a pretty woman? John thought dryly. Not a chance. That mind-set had gotten him nothing but trouble, was the cause of the mess he was now in.

What in the hell was he going to do?

The waitress returned with a brown bottle and a tall glass. She set them on the table, gave John a coy smile and a wink, then disappeared again into the crowd. John pushed the glass to one side, then took a deep swallow from the bottle.

Nasty, he thought, shuddering slightly. He really didn't like beer, but he wasn't about to start drinking hard liquor. He'd never be able to sort through the tangled maze in his mind if his brain was fuzzy from alcohol.

Maybe what he should do was quit thinking for a while, just zone out and observe the foolishness taking place around him. Yeah, that was the ticket. He would take a mental break, then square off against his dilemma again later. It was worth a try, might enable him to come up with a workable solution.

He shifted into a more comfortable position in the booth, then tapped his fingers against the cold bottle in an edgy, restless rhythm. He blanked his mind and watched the age-old mating games being played in an endless series of scenarios.

Half an hour later, the five-piece band appeared on the platform, tuned up, then exploded into loud music with a peppy number that caused a crush of humanity to flow onto the dance floor.

Several women approached John, but he refused each invitation to dance with a barely discernible shake of his head and a nondescript expression on his face.

He ordered another beer that he had no intention of drinking, figuring he'd better spend more money to justify occupying the booth.

Each time the reality of the situation that was plaguing him began to creep into the edges of his mind, he pushed it away, refusing to dwell on it during the mental hiatus he was allowing himself to take.

He simply sat there, as still as a statue, listening to the music, and people-watching.

Laura Bishop stood outside of Jake's Saloon, telling herself for the third time to open the door and enter the nightclub. She could hear the music and the muted sounds of voices and laughter that were beckoning to her.

A chill wind whipped across the parking lot, causing her to shiver and hunch into her jacket.

This was ridiculous, she told herself. She was standing there like an idiot, freezing to death, because she couldn't gather the courage to enter the dumb building.

She was acting like a silly child instead of a

twenty-nine-year-old woman. Granted, it was totally out of character for her to be out on the town by herself, let alone contemplating going into a bar, for heaven's sake.

Maybe she should just forget the whole thing, return to the ranch and curl up in front of the fire with the novel she'd been attempting to concentrate on.

Laura frowned as an image of the large, empty living room at the ranch flashed before her mental vision.

No, not tonight. She couldn't face the long, lonely hours in that house tonight. As the minutes on the clock had ticked slowly by, she'd become more and more depressed.

Her inner voice had been taunting her with a list of what she didn't have, would probably never have, causing an ache of loneliness to consume her, to grip her with icy tentacles.

Once she'd been accustomed to a busy schedule as social secretary to the four Royal Princesses of Wynborough. Now she had too many idle hours to fill each day.

Laura sighed.

The princesses. Each had found true love, her soul mate, and were all so blissfully happy. She was sincerely pleased that the four women, who were her friends as well as her employers, were floating on cloud nine as they began their new lives as the wives of the men they had chosen to be their life's partner.

But, oh, dear, how it all accentuated the stark reality that she was so very alone. Her few relation-

ships over the years had resulted in the frogs she'd
kissed remaining frogs, not one of them turning into
her Prince Charming.

Laura shivered as another gust of wind whipped
around her.

The air certainly held no promise of spring
warmth, that was for sure. She either had to hightail
it back to the ranch, or open the dumb door to the
nightclub and have an evening away from her solitude as she'd intended to do.

"Enough of this," she muttered. "My toes are
probably going to fall off if I stand here any longer.
Move, Laura. Right now."

She took a steadying breath, let it out slowly, then
yanked open the door and entered the building.

Despite the noise, smoky haze and the crush of
people, John's razor-sharp senses alerted him every
time the door to the club was opened and someone
new needed to be checked out. His appraisal was
done by rote, born of years of always being prepared
for potential danger.

He glanced at the door yet again, then did a double take as an attractive woman came into view. He
watched her hesitate, as though she was about to bolt
right back out of the crummy place. She swept her
gaze over the huge expanse in a jerky motion, her
eyes widening slightly at what she saw.

She was a fish out of water, John thought rather
absently. It didn't take a genius to realize that she
wasn't a regular on the barhopping scene. She

looked as if she was about to climb into a dentist's chair.

His ability to size people up quickly had saved his life on more than one occasion in the past, and there was no doubt in his mind that this woman was way out of her element in coming here on her own.

Well, she wouldn't be alone for long. She was pretty, in a fresh, wholesome sort of way. She had short blond hair that curled around her face, delicate features and very kissable lips. From this distance he couldn't discern the color of her eyes, though. Brown? Blue? Ah, hell, who cared? Forget it.

He shifted his attention back to the band, then seconds later found himself looking at the woman again.

She hadn't moved.

John chuckled and took a swig of beer.

Well, Pretty Lady, he thought, *how long are you going to stand there?* Ah, there she goes. She was unzipping her puffy blue jacket, apparently having decided to stay awhile.

Pink sweater. Nice. No, it wasn't exactly pink, it was that fancy color with the weird name. Mauve. Yeah, that was it. Okay, she had on a mauve sweater and jeans that were so new, they probably crackled when she walked.

So, Pretty Lady wasn't a true-blue Westerner. It was evident she hadn't washed those stiff, spanking new jeans a dozen times or more to soften them up and fade them a bit before she wore them.

She was, oh, maybe twenty-seven or twenty-eight,

but not single-scene savvy. She was definitely in foreign territory, and it showed like a brightly lit neon sign.

Pretty Lady had spunk, though. He'd give her that. She'd lifted her chin and started forward, making her way through the crowd at the bar. She'd probably faint dead out on her lovely face when she got over here and discovered there was nowhere to sit.

Man, John thought, shaking his head in self-disgust, he was really scrambling to keep his troubled thoughts at bay. He was actually wasting mental energy by concentrating on a city gal who had no business being in a Western bar where she didn't know the rules of the game.

"Hey, sweet thing," John heard a cowboy say as the man stepped in front of the woman. "I'm Pete. How about I buy you a drink?"

"Oh," she said. "No. No, thank you very much. If you'll excuse me, please, I'd like to go sit down and listen to the music."

"Fine with me," Pete said, placing one hand on her shoulder. "We'll sit together, dance some, have a couple of drinks."

"No," she said, removing his hand from her shoulder. "Thank you, but no."

Pete, John thought, *what part of "no" don't you understand?* That worn-out cliché had been custom-made for jerks like Pete.

"Now, darlin'," Pete said, shifting to slide his arm across the woman's shoulders, "you don't have to play hard to get with me. You're alone. I'm alone. We're a match made in heaven. Come on. Let's find us a table.''

''No,'' she said, attempting and failing to wiggle out of Pete's hold.

Pete leaned closer. ''Mmm. You smell real nice. Oh, yeah, you and I are going to get along just fine.''

''Let me go,'' she said, an echo of panic evident in her voice.

Don't you move, John told himself. He had his own troubles to contend with. Pretty Lady was getting her just deserts by walking into Jake's, and she'd have to handle it herself. It was none of his damn business.

''Lighten up, sugar,'' Pete said, kissing the woman on the temple.

''Stop it,'' she said, nearly shrieking.

Ah, hell, John thought. He should have stayed at the motel. He didn't need this hassle. But...ah, hell.

John slid out of the booth and pushed his way through the crowd in his path. He stopped in front of Pete and the woman.

''Pete,'' he said, his voice very low and very menacing, ''you have three seconds to take your arm off my woman. Are you hearing me, cowboy?''

''She's not your...'' Pete started, then met John's gaze. The color drained from Pete's face as he saw the ice in John's blue eyes and the tight set to his jaw. ''You bet.'' The cowboy dropped his arm from the woman's shoulders and took a step backward. ''Hey, man, my mistake.''

"You've got that straight," John said, then looked at the woman. "You're late. Car acting up again?"

"Car," she said, nodding. "Acting up. Again."

"Right," John said. "Come on, let's go, before someone takes the booth I have for us."

"Oh, I don't think—"

"No joke," John said gruffly. "That's very obvious."

He placed one large hand in the middle of her back and propelled her forward until they reached the booth. He shoved his jacket into the corner and glowered at her.

"Sit," he said.

Laura sank onto the leather bench and scooted into the middle, acutely aware that her legs were trembling so badly, they had been about to give way beneath her. She drew a shuddering breath, then looked directly at the man who was now sitting opposite her.

He pushed his Stetson up with one thumb and met her gaze.

Blue ice, Laura thought. His eyes were cold, like chips of blue ice. He wasn't handsome in a smooth, conventional manner; his features were far too rugged, with high cheekbones, a strong, square jaw and a straight blade of a nose.

His hair was dark brown, thick and shaggy, falling to his collar and badly in need of a trim. Broad shoulders strained against the material of his shirt, and his hands now wrapped around the bottle of beer were large and powerful appearing.

He was, without a doubt, the most earthy, rough-hewn—the most masculine—man she'd ever encountered. There was an aura of danger emanating from him, a sense of tension, of leashed strength that might explode at any moment.

Dear heaven, she thought, she could hardly breathe, and the wild tempo of her racing heart was echoing in her ears. Those eyes. Those incredible eyes of his were pinning her in place, making it impossible to move, to tear her gaze from his.

"I'm not going to gobble you up for dinner," he said, frowning. "You still look scared to death. I'm not the bad guy here, you know. I rescued you from Pete the Pest, remember?"

Laura folded her hands on the top of the table and managed to shift her eyes to her entwined fingers.

"Yes, I know," she said quietly, "and I want to thank you for what you did. I wasn't handling the situation with that man well at all." She sighed. "I never should have come here alone."

"Why did you?"

"I...I just couldn't face another long evening alone." She shook her head. "Listen to me. I don't go around baring my soul to perfect strangers." She met his gaze again. "I'm acting completely out of character tonight."

"Well, if it will make you feel any better, I'm not perfect, nor am I a stranger. I'm the knight who rode in on my white horse and saved you, the damsel in distress.

"And as far as baring your soul? I'm in this crummy place because *I* couldn't handle the four walls that were closing in on me. I needed to escape from my own thoughts. And I can't quite believe I'm telling you all this."

Laura smiled. "I guess we're both behaving out of character. I suppose the least we should do is introduce ourselves."

"No, wait," he said, raising one hand. "Since we're behaving so far from the norm, let's stick with first names only. That will make this whole thing not quite…well, real. I'm John."

"Hello, John. I'm Laura."

"Pretty name," he said, smiling slightly, "for a pretty lady."

Laura cocked her head to one side and studied John intently.

"You don't smile often, do you?" she said. "Your smiles just don't materialize naturally."

John lifted one shoulder in a shrug. "I've never thought about it," He paused. "No, I guess I don't have a hell of a lot to smile about."

The waitress appeared suddenly at the booth, startling both Laura and John.

"I see you took my advice, cowboy," she said, then looked at Laura. "Drink?"

"Just a cola, please," Laura said.

"You bet. Well, good-lookin'," she said to John, "you've got yourself a pretty woman, you're doin' some drinkin', so get out on the floor and do the dancin' part. You'll forget your troubles in no time at all. Be right back with the cola.''

John shook his head as the waitress hurried away.

''She probably actually believes that problems are that easily solved,'' he said.

''*Do* you have problems?'' Laura said.

''Doesn't everyone?'' John said, raising one eyebrow.

The waitress returned and slid a glass in front of Laura, then she disappeared again. Laura took a sip from the straw poking through the ice.

''Well,'' she said slowly, ''I suppose problems are subjective. One person could be upset because they couldn't find exactly the right shoes to match a new party dress. While another person could be in turmoil due to a serious illness they're suffering from. But each would say they had a problem.''

''Ah,'' John said, ''the lady is a heavy thinker, but what you're saying makes sense.'' He paused. ''Since we've agreed that tonight is a step away from reality, why don't you pretend you've known me for a long time and tell me your problems?''

As Laura looked at John, a strange warmth suffused her, a sense of peacefulness that was interwoven with a tingling excitement at being in close proximity to such a blatantly masculine man.

Yes, she thought, she could talk to John and he would listen, really hear, what she had to say. But she had a feeling that her woes fell into the category of the new shoes to match the party dress.

John appeared deeply troubled. There was fatigue etched on his ruggedly handsome face, and shifting emotions she couldn't define were reflected in the icy blue depths of his eyes. It was as though a massive weight was pressing on his broad, strong shoulders.

Oh, such fanciful ramblings. She was actually beginning to believe that she *did* know John well enough to sense that he was experiencing a great deal of inner turmoil, and that he needed her to share his crushing burden.

"Are we on equal terms, John?" she said. "I believe you keep your innermost feelings to yourself. I also think that you're a loner, a man who moves through life marching to the beat of his own drummer."

Laura smiled. "Don't ask me where all that came from, because I really don't know. I just feel very tuned in to you somehow." Her smile faded. "Are you going to be honest and open with me, if I am with you?"

Hell, no, John thought, taking a swig of the beer that was now distastefully warm. He didn't dump his problems on anyone...never had, never would.

He *was* a loner, just as Laura had pegged him. To have someone to share with required a man to belong, to fit in, and that just wasn't the way his deck was stacked.

But yet...

This woman, this Laura with the unknown last name, was reaching out to him, and for reasons he couldn't begin to understand he was starting to allow her to touch him deep within, could feel the warmth and gentleness of her caring.

Crazy. This whole conversation with Laura was nuts. He was succumbing to his bone-deep exhaustion and the tangled maze in his beleaguered brain. Hell, this was more than a *step* away from reality, it was a *world* apart from how he normally operated.

He should leave, just get up and walk out of there.

But he didn't want to, wasn't going to, and he was definitely losing his mind.

Ah, what the hell. Maybe if he talked about what he was facing, he could get a better handle on it, decide on a course of action.

That would sure as hell be a new way of doing things for him, but this night was different from any other...and so was pretty Laura. Oh, yes, so was Laura.

He nodded. "Okay. You've got a deal. We'll be honest and up front." A small smile tugged at the corners of his lips. "After all, we've known each other for years. Right?"

Their eyes met and the music and noise of the crowd faded into oblivion. They were encased in a sudden hazy mist that swirled around them, dipping, stroking, heightening awareness of the other and causing embers of desire to begin to glow deep within them.

"Right," Laura whispered, unable to tear her gaze from John's. "I've known you for years and years, John."

He nodded slowly, attempting and failing to ignore the coiling heat low in his body, and the increased tempo of his heart.

Lust? he thought, in self-disgust. He was no better than Pete the Pest. Worse yet was the fact that Laura wasn't even his type.

She hadn't come into Jake's looking for a man, hadn't been on the prowl like the other women who knew the rules and how to play the game. Lust. He could feel his body reacting to Laura. What a sleaze-ball he was.

But maybe…yeah, maybe, this wasn't lust in its usual form. He and Laura were connecting in a place they had invented just for themselves, for these few hours stolen out of time.

They were caring, sharing, being there for each other in their loneliness, fulfilling needs. This heat thrumming low in his body might be…desire, an honest, more gentle wanting, something he'd never experienced before.

That made sense. Sure. There was a special quality to this interlude with Laura. It stood to reason that new and different emotions would rise to the fore. He was being transported somewhere he'd never been. So be it.

"Who are you, Laura?" he said, his voice slightly husky.

"I…" Laura started, then drew a much-needed breath. "I'm a very ordinary person. I grew up in Michigan in a loving family. I have an older sister,

Linda, who is married. We're very close, friends as well as sisters.

"I went to Michigan State and got degrees in business and public relations. For the past five years I've had a marvelous position as social secretary for the daughters of a prominent family." She shrugged. "That's it."

"Why are you in Hope, Arizona, of all places?"

"I'm completing an assignment connected to my job. Tonight...well, I'm just not accustomed to having so many idle hours and I was restless, just couldn't sit still for another second."

"And you were lonely," John said quietly.

Laura took a sip of her drink, then looked at John again.

"Yes," she said, lifting her chin. "Since we agreed to be honest with each other, I'll admit I was very lonely tonight. My life suddenly seemed empty, with no...no rainbow in my future."

"Rainbow?" he said, raising his eyebrows. "What do you want to find at the end of that rainbow? The ever-famous pot of gold?"

"No." Laura shook her head. "Happiness. A special man, my soul mate, to share my life, to have babies with. See? I told you I was a very ordinary person. Nothing fancy."

"You're not ordinary, Laura. You're special. You're honest, real, like a breath of fresh air."

Man, John thought, where was this stuff coming from? He didn't say junk like this to women, like some corny would-be poet or whatever. But he meant it. Laura was special, rare, and he was very glad she'd walked into Jake's Saloon tonight.

"Thank you," Laura said, smiling. "That's a lovely thing to say." Her smile faded. "Now it's your turn, John. I'm here. I'm listening. Talk to me."

Chapter Two

Laura watched John as he jerked his head around to stare at the band, then the bottle of beer in front of him, then at a point somewhere above her head.

He was getting cold feet, she thought, shrugging out of her jacket. John was warring with himself, deciding if he was actually going to keep his half of their agreement.

She could understand his hesitation. It would be very difficult for a man like John to reveal his innermost thoughts.

But he would do it, she just somehow knew that he would, because he was a man of his word.

She felt so connected to John, as though they really had known each other for many years. How strange all of this was. Yet it was wonderful, too.

Yes, John would talk to her, share with her, when he was ready. She would simply wait patiently... wait for John.

A silent minute ticked by. Then two. Three.

John cleared his throat and shifted his gaze slowly to meet Laura's.

"I grew up in Hope," he said quietly, "but I never felt as though I belonged here. I left as soon as I was old enough. That's my fault, the sense of not fitting in, not my family's. They're good people."

Laura nodded, her eyes riveted on John's.

"My family doesn't know that I'm back. I checked into a motel because I needed some time alone, to figure out what I'm going to do about..." John stopped speaking and shook his head. "Hell."

Laura reached across the table and covered one of John's hands with one of hers as she leaned toward him.

"Going to do about what?" she said. "What's wrong, John?"

John turned his hand over and grasped Laura's. Heat shimmered up her arm, across her breasts, then began to swirl throughout her. She could feel a warm flush stain her cheeks, but made no attempt to free her hand from John's hold.

So strong, she thought, yet so gentle.

"The last time I was home," John said, looking directly at her again, "I came here, to Jake's, met up with a woman I knew and we spent the night together. We both understood there were no strings attached. It was just...well, a night.''

''I understand,'' Laura said.

''A couple of days ago I received a letter from a friend of that woman,'' John continued. ''It had taken quite a while for the letter to reach me because I was out of the country. The letter said that the woman I knew had died several months before.''

''Oh, my goodness,'' Laura said.

''Yeah, well, there's more,'' John said, his grip on Laura's hand tightening slightly. ''The woman had...she never told me, but...'' He shook his head.

''John?'' Laura said.

''She had my baby, Laura,'' he said, his voice gritty with emotion. ''My son. She hadn't planned on telling me, nor making any demands on me, but then she died.

''Her friend took the baby and started the process of finding me to tell me I had a son, that I needed to be his father because he no longer had a mother. He doesn't have anyone.''

''Dear heaven,'' Laura whispered. ''A baby. You have a son who needs you to make a home for him, to raise him and—how old is he now?''

''Eleven months. He's going to celebrate his first birthday pretty soon. His name is Jeremiah.''

''Have you seen him?''

''No.'' John frowned. ''I spoke with the woman on the phone and told her I'd pick Jeremiah up to-morrow. I needed some sleep and a plan for—ah hell, Laura, what am I going to do? How can a man like me raise a son?''

Sudden tears stung Laura's eyes as she saw the raw pain on John's face, heard it in his voice. She wanted to close the distance between them, hug him, hold him, tell him he wasn't alone.

''A man like you?'' she said, blinking away the unwelcome tears. ''You're saying that in such a derogatory manner, and you shouldn't. You're warm and caring. You were the one, the only one, who stepped in and rescued me from that aggressive man.

''You're holding my hand, John, and you could crush it with very little effort, but I know my hand is safe. I know that *I'm* safe with you, because your strength is tempered with infinite gentleness.

''How can a man like you raise a son? By just being you, by loving Jeremiah with all your heart. You're his father, and I think he's a lucky little boy to have you.''

''Thank you, Laura,'' John said. ''More than I can even express in words.'' He drew a shuddering breath and let it out slowly. ''I guess all I can do is the best I can do. Man, I've never even held a baby before, let alone… I suppose there are books I can read about child care or something.''

Laura nodded. ''You can use books as a guideline, but don't expect Jeremiah to do exactly what is described. Babies are people in small bodies. They have personalities, likes, dislikes, just as adults do. You'll need to follow your own instincts.''

John chuckled, the rumbly, male sound causing a shiver to course through Laura.

"You're assuming that I *have* some paternal instincts," he said, smiling. "If I do, they're news to me."

Laura matched his smile. "They're there. Trust me. No, correct that. Trust and believe in *yourself,* Daddy."

John's smile faded. "Daddy. Father. Whew. I guess it's really sinking in that I have a son." He paused. "I wonder if he looks like me? Do year-old babies talk? Walk?" He laughed. "Play poker?"

"Oh, it's so good to hear you laugh," Laura said, "see you smile."

"Well, I wouldn't be if it weren't for you, Laura. I'm very glad that you got cabin fever and came to Jake's tonight."

"So am I," she said softly.

They smiled, warm smiles, meaningful smiles, smiles that wrapped around them like a comforting blanket.

Then the smiles disappeared as they continued to gaze into each other's eyes. The desire within them burned brighter, hotter, consumed them.

And they welcomed it, because it was real and rich, and so very, very right. It belonged to them in their private and special world.

They communicated without words, messages of want and need sent and received with intertwined emotions of peacefulness and excitement.

John slid out of the booth and extended his hand

to Laura. She placed her hand in his with no hesitation and moved to stand by his side. He retrieved their jackets, assisted Laura in putting hers on, shrugged into his own, then dropped several bills onto the table.

With his hand resting on Laura's back, they made their way through the crowd at the bar to emerge into the clear, cold night.

"I walked over from my motel," John said quietly. "It's a couple of miles from here."

"I borrowed a vehicle from where I'm staying," Laura said. "We can go in that."

John stepped in front of her and placed his hands on her shoulders.

"Laura." He looked directly into her eyes, able to see her in the light from the neon sign on the building. "I want you to know that this isn't just…just a night like I spoke of before."

"I know that, John," she said softly. "I don't quite understand why this is so right, but it is, and I'll have no regrets about what we're going to share. I promise you that."

He nodded, brushed his lips over hers, then tugged his Stetson low on his forehead.

A short time later, John parked the truck Laura had borrowed in front of his room at the motel. He'd left a small lamp on and the room welcomed them with a dim, golden glow.

John closed the door and slipped the chain into

place. Laura leaned against the door and he braced his hands on either side of her head.

"I can't see you after tonight," he said. "I have to focus on my son, on learning how to become the best father I can be."

"I understand," she said, nodding. "It's better this way, because I'm only here temporarily. This is our night, John. It was fate, our meeting at Jake's, talking, sharing, feeling as though we'd known each other for a very long time. It's all very special, rare, and very, very beautiful."

John nodded, then lowered his head to claim Laura's mouth in a gentle, fleeting kiss.

Laura kept her arms at her sides as he kissed her again, deeper this time, parting her lips to seek, find, then duel with her tongue in the sweet darkness of her mouth.

Laura's legs began to tremble and she gripped John's jacket, holding fast.

The kiss went on and on.

It was magic.

It was a night stolen out of time and reality.

It was clothes seeming to float away by a wish, instead of a touch, as desire exploded within them with hot, licking flames. It was passion soaring to previously unknown, glorious heights.

Cool sheets on the bed greeted their heated bodies and they kissed, caressed, explored, marveling at the wonders discovered.

John supported his weight on one forearm as he

skimmed his other hand over Laura's breasts, then on to splay over her flat stomach.

"You're beautiful, Laura," he murmured, close to her lips.

"So are you," she whispered, her fingertips tracing the taut muscles in his back.

He shifted lower to lave the nipple of one of her breasts with his tongue. Laura sank her hands into his thick hair, pressing his mouth harder onto the soft flesh. She closed her eyes for a moment to savor the exquisite sensations rushing through her.

She opened her eyes again, wanting to see John in the glow of the lamp, wanting to memorize every detail of him, cherishing the sight, the sound, the taste and feel of this magnificent man.

Her man, Laura thought dreamily. Hers for one night. They were creating memories together that she would keep forever, tuck away so securely in her heart. In the years yet to come she could reach into the secret cupboard and relive the magic of this night.

"Magic," she said, not realizing she'd spoken aloud.

"Yes," John said, raising his head to meet her gaze. "That's what it is—*was* from the moment I saw you. I've never talked, shared, with anyone the way I have with you, probably never will again. Thank you, Laura, for…for just being you."

"And I thank you, John, for being you, for chasing away my loneliness, for trusting me with your worries and fears, the very essence of who you are. I'll never forget you. Never.''

''Yes, you will, and you should.''

''No, I...''

''Shh,'' he said, then his mouth melted over hers.

They were no longer in a small, shabby room; they were in a field of wildflowers under a brilliant blue sky and a warming sun. They were in a place meant only for the two of them, where no one else was allowed to go.

Their place. Their world. Their magic.

Their breathing became labored and hearts thundered. Hands were never still and where hands had traveled, lips followed in a heated path.

It was wild, and reckless, and wonderful.

''John,'' Laura gasped finally, ''please.''

''Yes,'' he said, his voice hoarse. ''Wait. I want to protect you.''

John returned to her as quickly as possible and Laura reached out for him eagerly, his absence having been an eternity.

John moved over her, catching his weight on his arms, then he entered her slowly, filling her, watching her face for any hint of pain.

Laura sighed in pure feminine pleasure, a soft smile forming on her lips. She raised her hips to meet him and the dance began, building in power and force to a pounding rhythm, taking them higher and higher.

Reaching. Glorying in the ecstasy. Anticipating

the moment of exquisite release. Giving and receiving in total abandon.

On and on...

"John!"

"Yes!"

Laura clung to his shoulders and he flung his head back, a groan rumbling deep in his chest. They were there, together, and neither wished the moment to end. They hovered, savoring, awed by the splendor.

John collapsed against Laura, his energy spent. He rolled off of her quickly so as not to crush her, then he nestled her close to his side.

Hearts quieted. Bodies cooled. The flames of desire dimmed to simmering embers.

They didn't speak as the magic demanded silence. Reverently, carefully, memories were hidden away in private chambers of their hearts.

They slept, heads on the same pillow, Laura's hand encircling a small ring that hung on a chain around John's neck.

Fingers of sunlight inched beneath the curtains on the window to tiptoe across Laura's face, waking her. She opened her eyes slowly, then in the next instant sat bolt upright on the bed, her heart racing as she realized she had absolutely no idea where she was.

The cobwebs of sleep disappeared with a blink, to be replaced by vivid images of the previous night...and John.

Laura glanced around the small room, then saw a

scrap of paper on one of the bed pillows. She snatched it up and read the message written in a bold, sprawling handwriting.

Laura—
I hope you find your rainbow. You deserve it.
                                         John

Laura sank back against the pillows and reread the note three more times.

John, her mind whispered. He'd remembered what she'd said about wishing to find the rainbow that would bring her the true happiness she was seeking. She had spoken and he had listened, really heard what she had said.

John, her man of the magical night. He was so magnificent, strong yet gentle, so sensitive and caring.

John, who was facing the tremendous challenge of raising a son he hadn't even known he had. He'd trusted her enough to share his fears with her, his feelings of inadequacy regarding his new, daunting and awe-evoking role.

John. Their lovemaking had been so exquisitely beautiful, it was beyond description. Magic. In the world they'd created together, every touch and kiss had been ecstasy. They had moved as one, a single entity, their dance of love so synchronized and perfect, it was as though they'd been lovers for years, knew every nuance of the other.

''John,'' Laura whispered, then sighed.

She had no regrets about her rash actions of last night. None. The only shadow hovering over her was the realization that she would never see John again. She'd known that at the outset, but still…

No, no, she had to be sophisticated and mature about this. Facts were facts. And memories were memories, hers to keep.

"Goodbye, John," Laura said softly, as she clutched the note. "Thank you."

She showered and dressed, then after one last look at the shabby little room, she closed the door behind her with a quiet click. She turned away from this magical place, blinked away sudden and unwelcome tears, lifted her chin and prepared to drive back to the ranch.

Alone.

During the fifteen miles she had to cover to reach The Rocking C Ranch, Laura gave herself a continuous, stern lecture.

Before she even entered the house, she decreed, she would have pushed the memories of John to a safe corner of her mind, would not allow him to step through the front door with her, to haunt her with his sensuous presence.

The long hours she spent in that house waiting to fulfill her assignment were difficult enough without aching for the sight, the sound, the taste and touch of a man she would never see again.

"Go away, John," she said, flapping one hand in

the air as the house came into view. "Oh, please, just go away right now."

The house was a large, one-story traditional ranch style, with five bedrooms and a huge, modern kitchen. The living room that Laura entered boasted an enormous flagstone fireplace on one wall, gleaming hardwood floors with a scattering of Native American area rugs, and oversize dark wood furniture done in varying shades of tweed.

Laura hurried to the bedroom she was using during her stay, not wishing to see Betty, the housekeeper. Betty was a no-nonsense woman in her midfifties, who would not hesitate to ask where she had spent the night.

Answering that question, Laura decided as she changed into fresh clothes, could hopefully be avoided if Betty didn't have a clue that Laura hadn't been tucked in her own bed.

Laura left her bedroom and peered into the kitchen, breathing a sigh of relief when she saw it was empty, then headed for the pot of prepared coffee. She settled at the big oak table with a mug of the steaming brew.

And thought about John.

"Would you stop that?" she said, smacking the top of the table with the palm of one hand. "Just cut it out. Get a grip. Right now."

"Who are you talking to?"

Laura jerked in her chair as Betty entered the kitchen from the mudroom beyond. She was carrying a basket of eggs and wearing her usual jeans, boots and Western shirt. She was tall, slender and her short gray hair curled around her attractive face.

"Me," Laura said with a sigh.

Betty laughed. "You're certainly giving yourself what-for this morning." She went to the sink and began to rinse off the eggs. "Sleep well?"

"Oh, I...you bet," Laura said, feeling a warm flush creep onto her cheeks.

"Then why the grumpy mood?" Betty said, glancing over at her, then resuming her chore.

"I'm just dreading facing another long day, I guess," Laura said. "I've only been here alone a short time, but it seems like a year. The thing is, I have no idea how many more days I'll need to remain. Heaven only knows when John Colton will decide to make a trip home for a visit. I have to sit here and wait until he shows up."

"Well, there's worse places to be than on the Colton ranch." Betty paused and shook her head. "I still find it hard to believe that our John might actually be Prince James Wyndham of Wynborough.

"When the Coltons adopted him as a baby, there wasn't a clue about his identity. He was just left on the doorstep of The Sunshine Home for Children. John is in for a mighty big shock when he does come home."

"I should have asked you this before, Betty, but how do you think John will feel about this news?"

"No telling," Betty said, shutting off the water in the sink. "John is impossible to predict. He's a

Colton, but he never has thought and acted like one.''

''Well, he really isn't a Colton. He's a Wyndham.''

''As far as his parents and his brother, Mitch, are concerned, he's a Colton,'' Betty said decisively. ''They love him as their own. That will never change, no matter what new fancy name and title John has. A prince. Good gracious, wonders never cease.''

''A prince who was kidnapped as an infant and believed to be dead all these years,'' Laura said. ''And I'm the one who has been assigned the nifty task of explaining his true identity to him. I hope he doesn't get into a kill-the-messenger mode.''

''Now there's a thought,'' Betty said with a burst of laughter.

''Thanks a bunch,'' Laura said, smiling.

''Well, I'm off to The Triple Bar,'' Betty said, placing the eggs in the refrigerator. She removed a covered dish and bumped the refrigerator door closed with her hip. ''Jolene is laid up with a broken ankle, and I'm taking a casserole over for their supper. I'll be gone the better part of the day, I imagine, because Jolene loves to chatter.''

''It's nice of you to keep her company, and I'm sure her family will appreciate having one of your delicious casseroles for their supper.''

''Well, I'll see you later. Oh, and, Laura? The next time you stay out all night, turn off your bedroom light before you leave, would you? No sense in running up the electric bill for no reason.''

''Oh, good grief.'' Laura plunked one elbow on the table and rested her forehead in her hand. ''How embarrassing. How mortifying. How…''

''Normal,'' Betty finished for her. ''There's no shame in being a healthy young woman with wants and needs. I just couldn't resist taking a poke at you, but I'm certainly not passing judgment. In fact, I'm more inclined to say good for you. I'll see you when I get back.''

'''Bye,'' Laura mumbled.

A heavy silence fell over the room and Laura drained her coffee mug quickly, wishing to escape from the sudden chill of loneliness that dropped over her like a dark cloud.

She spent the next hour writing breezy letters to her parents, her sister, Linda, and her best friend since childhood, Olivia, who was now a busy mother of four back in Michigan.

In none of the letters was there one word about Laura's magical night with John.

No, she thought, placing the stamp on the third envelope. Those memories were hers alone. She'd keep them tucked safely in her heart for all time.

Maybe when she was old and gray, she'd sit in a rocking chair and tell Olivia and Linda about the magnificent man who had touched her life so briefly, but so deeply.

But not now. No, not now.

Laura wandered up to the main road fronting the

ranch and put the letters in the mailbox to be picked up by the rural delivery man. Thunder rumbled in the distance and dark clouds edged the horizon.

Back in the house, she switched her cotton blouse for a red sweater, which she wore over gray corduroy slacks, then she made a fire in the hearth in the living room.

Settling into one of the big, comfortable chairs by the fireplace, she actually managed to become engrossed in the mystery novel she was reading.

An hour later, a sharp knock sounded at the front door and Laura jerked at the sudden noise.

She hadn't heard a vehicle approach the house, she thought, settling the book on the table next to the chair. Maybe one of the ranch hands was looking for Betty.

She got to her feet.

But the men used the mudroom door, she remembered, as she crossed the room. Maybe she'd been concentrating so much on her book that she hadn't heard a knock on the rear door. And the thunder was still rumbling noisily so...well, whatever.

Laura opened the door with a pleasant expression on her face.

Then she stopped breathing as a gasp caught in her throat.

Standing before her, with a blanket-covered bundle on his shoulder, was John.

John, her mind hammered in disbelief. Her man of the magical night. Magnificent, tall, powerful, sensitive, compelling John was staring right at her with a shocked expression on his face.

Dear heaven, how had he found her? What was he doing here?

Chapter Three

John felt as though he'd been punched in the gut as he stared at Laura, who was staring at him.

His first thought when Laura had appeared in the doorway was that he was imagining she was there.

He'd written her a short, heartfelt note that morning, then stood next to the bed in the motel, losing track of time as he'd watched her sleep. He hadn't wanted to leave that room, leave Laura and the magic they'd created together.

Their lovemaking had been fantastic, far beyond the usual physical release. He had made love *with* a woman, not *to* a woman, the union being intertwined with emotions, some of which he couldn't identify. Incredible.

It had taken every bit of willpower he possessed

to finally turn and walk out of that room. He'd emerged into the crisp morning air and closed the door behind him with a quiet click.

Then reality had slammed against him. He was about to see his son—*his son*—for the first time. He would take responsibility for that baby, then begin a life-style that was so foreign and so damn frightening.

Laura's words of the previous night echoed in his head as he'd driven the miles to where Jeremiah was waiting for him. He'd clung to what Laura had said like a lifeline, hearing her state so sincerely that he would do fine in his role of father by just being himself and following his paternal instincts.

Laura. She was so pretty, real and honest, so caring. He had bared his soul to her, and it had felt so right to share his innermost feelings and fears.

Laura was special. What they'd shared in those stolen hours had been like nothing he'd experienced before. But he'd had to let her go to concentrate entirely on his son and *their* future together.

And now?

Laura was honest-to-God standing two feet in front of him.

What in the hell was she doing here?

"What are you..." Laura and John said in unison.

They stopped speaking and both frowned.

"This is crazy," John said gruffly. "What are you doing on The Rocking C?"

"I live here," Laura said, amazed that she could still speak. "Sort of."

"*You* live here?" he said. "*I* live here. Sort of."
He paused and shook his head. "Damn it, Laura,
this is my family's ranch, the Colton spread. I'm
John Colton."

"Oh...my...God," Laura whispered, her eyes
widening. "You're John Colton? Oh, dear heaven.
John Colton? Oh, good grief."

"You're very articulate, Laura. Would you mind
telling me who *you* are?" John narrowed his eyes.
"Are you my brother's wife, or whatever?"

"No, of course not. That's insulting, considering
that you and I... Never mind. I'm Laura Bishop and
I—you're John Colton?"

"Would you cut that out?" he said, none too quietly. The blanket-covered bundle he was holding
stirred. "Oh, man, I'm waking him up."

"That's Jeremiah," Laura said breathlessly.
"That's your son."

"Bingo. Would it meet with your approval, Ms.
Bishop, if I came into *my* house?"

"Oh. Oh. Yes, of course." Laura stepped back
quickly to allow John to enter the house. "I'm sorry,
very sorry. Come in."

John strode into the living room, shooting Laura
a dark glare as he passed her. He went to the sofa
facing the fireplace and eased the baby slowly from
his shoulder, placing him on the soft cushions. Jeremiah wiggled, then stilled, as he slept on.

On trembling legs, Laura moved to stand next to
John. She looked at the sleeping baby and her breath
caught.

Jeremiah was a miniature John, she thought incredulously, feeling a funny little tug on her heart. The baby had the same silky dark brown hair, straight nose, square little jaw as his father. This was Jeremiah, John's son.

And this magnificent man of the magical night, she thought frantically, sliding a glance at John, was John Colton, or rather, heaven help her, Prince James Wyndham of Wynborough.

John took off his jacket and Stetson, tossed them onto a chair, then crossed his arms over his chest and frowned at Laura, who was staring at the baby again.

"Oh, John," she said softly, "Jeremiah is so beautiful. What a *wonderful* son you have."

"He's not the subject at the moment. *You* have some explaining to do," John said, "and this better be good. My first question is, where is my brother, Mitch? Is he out on the range working? And where's Betty?"

"That's three questions," Laura said, smiling weakly as she shifted her attention to him. "Sorry," she added quickly, as John's frown deepened. "I was just attempting to lighten things up a tad."

She hurried over to the chair where she'd been reading so peacefully an eternity ago, and sank onto it gratefully.

"You have to realize, John," she said, "that your suddenly appearing here, your being who you are, is a tremendous shock to me."

"No more than my finding you in my family's

home.'' He dragged a restless hand through his hair.
''Let's start at the top. Why are you here?''

''Maybe you should sit down.''

''No.''

''Please?'' Laura said.

''Hell,'' John said, then slouched onto the chair
opposite her.

Laura clutched her hands tightly in her lap, then
drew a steadying breath.

''John,'' she said, ''do you remember my telling
you that I work for a prominent family and was in
Hope to complete an assignment?''

John propped his elbows on the arms of the chair,
then made a steeple of his fingers which he rested
lightly against his lips.

''I remember,'' he said. ''So?''

''So, the assignment was to wait here on The
Rocking C until you, until John Colton, returned
home for a visit.''

''Well, I'm here in living, breathing color. What
do you want me for?''

''I'm...I'm supposed to tell you...that is, it's
been discovered that... What I'm trying to say is...''

''Damn it, Laura,'' John said, then glanced
quickly at Jeremiah. ''Just spit it out, would you?''

Laura lifted her chin. ''John, you were kidnapped
as an infant and believed, by your family, to be
dead. You were left at The Sunshine Home for Children, and adopted by the Coltons.''

John narrowed his eyes but didn't speak.

''As unbelievable as this may sound, we strongly

suspect you are Prince James Wyndham of Wynborough, the biological son and heir of King Phillip and Queen Gabriella. There. I did it. I told you.''

A grin slowly began to appear on John's face, then grew bigger. He slid his hands to the back of his head and chuckled.

"Mitch cooked this up, right?" he said. "He decided I'd been away too long and was due to visit the old homestead. Man, he really outdid himself with this nonsense. Where is he? I want to tell him to his face that I didn't buy into this for a second. A prince, huh? That's rich. My big brother has a hell of an imagination.''

"John," Laura said quietly, "every word I've said is true. I swear to you that it is. You are Prince James Wyndham of Wynborough." She paused. "We recently learned of a blanket that was with you when you were left at The Sunshine Home, a blanket with the royal crest on it and—"

"Wait a minute," John said, raising one hand from behind his head. "A crest? What kind? What does it look like?"

"I'll show you," Laura said, getting to her feet. "I have some stationery with the Wyndham crest embossed on the top.''

Laura hurried to her room and returned with a sheet of expensive paper, which she handed to John. She sat back down, her gaze riveted on John as he stared at the crest on the paper.

After a few tension-filled moments, he pulled the chain he wore around his neck free of his shirt and looked at the tiny ring attached. He shifted his eyes to the paper, then back to the ring.

Laura felt a warm flush stain her cheeks as she remembered grasping that small ring while making love with John. She'd held in her hand the *proof* that John Colton was Prince James Wyndham.

"No," he said, lunging to his feet. "Mitch knows I was wearing this ring when I was abandoned. He's seen it often enough to have this stationery printed up as part of the joke."

Laura sighed. "Call around. Discover for yourself if there is a place named Wynborough, if the heir to the throne was kidnapped as a baby, and ask what the Wyndham family crest looks like. Go ahead, John, do it. You obviously aren't going to believe *me*."

John sat back down in the chair and propped his elbows on his knees, lacing his fingers together loosely. He stared at Laura, studying her intently, as though he was attempting to peer inside her head. She met his gaze directly as she lifted her chin.

"John," she said finally, splaying one hand on her chest, "this is me, Laura. I'm the same woman I was last night, the one who shared...shared so much with you. I wouldn't lie to you, John. Somewhere, deep inside you, you know that."

Several seconds ticked by in heavy silence, then John shook his head and leaned back in the chair, staring up at the ceiling.

"No," he said, "you wouldn't lie to me." He looked at Laura again. "All right, I believe you, but it's just too much to deal with. I have enough on my plate with finding out that I'm a father. Jeremiah comes first. What you've told me has to go on the back burner for now.''

"But—''

"No, I don't want to discuss it any further at the moment. Don't push me on this, Laura. I can only handle so much at once.'' He paused. "Where's Mitch?''

"Oh, dear,'' Laura said. "Well, Mitch married Alexandra Wyndham, the eldest princess of Wynborough, your…your sister. They're expecting a baby. The whole family is in Wynborough for the marriage of Elizabeth, another one of your sisters, to Rafe Thorton, who is actually Prince Raphael of Thortonburg. I stayed here on The Rocking C to wait for your return home.''

"Oh, man,'' John said, shaking his head. "I'm Prince James of wherever. Mitch has married a princess, who is actually my sister and—well, forget it. My brain is on overload and I've had enough of this.''

Thunder rumbled across the sky.

John got to his feet. "I have to unload Jeremiah's stuff from the back of the truck before it starts to rain.'' He started toward the door, then stopped. "Watch Jeremiah, will you?''

"Yes. Yes, of course, I will.''

As John disappeared out the front door, Laura moved to sit on the end cushion of the sofa, a soft smile forming on her lips as she stared at the sleeping baby.

His hands were splayed on either side of his head and his lips were slightly parted. He was dressed in blue corduroy overalls, a faded red jersey and a pair of white socks with a hole in one toe.

"Hello, Jeremiah," Laura whispered.

Oh, she wanted to scoop him up, she thought wistfully. She'd inhale his special baby aroma as she held that sturdy little body close and safe. He'd done nothing more than sleep in baby innocence and he was already staking a claim on her heart.

John made numerous trips between the house and the truck, producing a dismantled white crib, mattress, a tattered car seat, high chair, several cardboard boxes and two paper sacks.

As he slid the last box into place, it skidded into the pieces of the crib that were propped against the wall, causing them to slide down onto the hardwood floor with a loud crash.

Jeremiah jerked, opened his eyes, took one look at Laura and cut loose with an earsplitting wail.

John spun around. "What did you do to him?"

"Nothing," Laura said, jumping to her feet. "It was you, making all that racket. You woke him up out of a sound sleep and it frightened him." She looked at the baby. "Shh, shh. It's okay. Don't cry."

John strode to the back of the sofa, reached over and picked up Jeremiah, nestling him against his broad shoulder. The baby quieted, then stuck his thumb in his mouth.

Laura smiled. "Well, look at that. You have a father's touch."

"Yeah, right," John said, frowning.

Jeremiah popped his thumb out of his mouth and grabbed John's nose. The baby gurgled happily.

"Like my nose, sport?" John said, smiling. "It's a handy toy, huh? Sticking right out there for you."

"He's so adorable," Laura said with a sigh.

"Yep, he's cute."

"He looks exactly like you, John."

"Think so?" he said, obviously pleased with the statement.

"Oh, heavens, yes. He's a miniature...you." Laura paused and frowned. "Where's his jacket?"

John frowned again as Jeremiah continued to pat, then grab, his daddy's nose.

"He doesn't have a jacket," John said. "He doesn't even have a pair of shoes. His crib is a piece of junk and...I feel so damn guilty that he doesn't have decent stuff."

"I don't think you should swear like that in front of him, John. He's at the age where he'll start parroting what he hears."

"Oh. Right. No swearing. But, hell—I mean, heck—he needs a new crib, clothes, toys. Look at the car seat. It's a mess, probably wouldn't even pass the safety codes." He paused. "Uh-oh."

"What's wrong?" Laura said.

"He may be beating my nose to death, but it still works. Jeremiah needs his diaper changed."

"That's nice," Laura said pleasantly. "Go for it."

"Me?" he said, his eyes widening. "I've never changed a baby's diaper."

Laura threw out her arms. "Neither have I. I've spent time with my sister's kids and my friend Olivia's little ones, but I never changed a diaper on any of them."

"Where's Betty?" John said, a slight edge of panic in his voice.

"She's gone to The Triple Bar and expects to be away most of the day."

"Ah, hell!"

"John, watch your mouth!"

Jeremiah took exception to the loud exchange and burst into tears.

Laura came to where John stood holding the wailing baby. She placed her hand on Jeremiah's back at the exact moment John moved his hand to do the same. John's hand covered Laura's and she snapped her head up to meet his gaze.

Jeremiah drew a shuddering breath, then stuck his thumb in his mouth.

Laura and John didn't move. They stood there, hands layered on the baby's back, memories of the previous night rushing over them in a sensuous cascade of vivid images.

Their hearts began to beat in a rapid tempo as heat swirled and tightened low in their bodies. Desire seemed to hum through the air with an ever-increasing intensity, weaving around and through them.

"No," John said, jerking his hand away.

"What?" Laura blinked, bringing herself back from the hazy, passion-laden place she'd floated to.

John took a step backward and shook his head. "No, Laura. I told you last night that I couldn't see you again, that I had to concentrate entirely on Jeremiah. The fact that you're here, on The Rocking C, doesn't change that. We have to pretend, behave—whatever—as though last night never happened."

"I understand," she said quietly, wrapping her hands around her elbows. "Yes, of course. You're right."

"Good. Fine." John paused and sighed. "Look, I don't mean to sound like an unfeeling son of a—" he glanced quickly at Jeremiah "—gun, but this is the way it has to be. My son deserves my full attention."

Laura nodded, inwardly fuming at herself for the devastating sense of rejection she was registering, along with a chill of loneliness.

She knew, darn it, she knew that what John was saying was the way it had to be, was the sensible, agreed-upon plan. They'd had their magical night together and hadn't expected ever to cross paths again. She knew that.

But, oh, it hurt so much to see John step away

from her, to erect a nearly tangible wall between them.

Laura, please, she mentally begged, *get a grip.* She had to regain control of her raging emotions before she burst into tears and made a complete fool of herself.

''No problem, John,'' she said, hoping her voice was steadier than it sounded to her own ears. ''It's just a crazy coincidence that we even saw each other again. Last night happened, it's over, so be it. There's no reason to think about it again.''

The hell there isn't, John thought. Their night... all of it, every moment...the talking, sharing, the lovemaking, had been incredible, beyond belief. Laura was dismissing it all as no big deal? How could she do that? How could she just—

Damn it, Colton, he rebuked himself. Laura was doing exactly what he said *he* was. He'd just told her that their time together had to be forgotten even though they were both there at the ranch.

But, oh, man, he wanted to pull Laura into his arms, kiss her, taste her, feel her slender body pressed to his. He wanted to make love with her until they were both too exhausted to move. He wanted to experience the magic again...with Laura.

Jeremiah wiggled and began to whine, and John looked at his son.

He wanted to hold Laura in his arms? he thought. There was no room for her there, because he was holding this defenseless child who had no one to take care of him, to love him, except a father who didn't even know how to change a diaper.

No, there was no place for Laura in his life. No space, emotionally or physically, for anyone but Jeremiah.

"All right," John said, then cleared his throat. "We understand each other then. I focus on my son. You do...whatever it is that you do."

"I'll be contacting the royal family in Wynborough," Laura said coolly, "and informing them that you've returned and now know the facts of your true identity, your heritage."

"Ah, Laura, don't do that," he said, frowning. "I don't have the time, or mental energy, to think about what you told me. I don't want those people descending on me like a pack of vultures."

"Those people," Laura said, her volume on high again, "are your family. They are *not* a pack of vultures, as you so crudely put it."

"No, Laura, my family includes my son, my brother, Mitch, and my parents, Robert and Cissy Colton. That's it. End of story. I don't want anything to do with your fancy king and queen, and princesses, or with being a prince, for Pete's sake. I'm John Colton. Got that?"

"John, would you think about the Wyndhams' feelings for one moment? They thought you were dead. Oh, can't you understand what it will mean to them to know you as you now are, welcome you into their—"

"No," he interrupted. "It's too late. I've gotten

along just fine without them. My son is what matters most. I'm concentrating on Jeremiah. That's it. No one else is important. No one.''

Laura cringed, feeling as though she'd been struck by a physical blow. It was there again, the pain of rejection, the chill of loneliness.

No one else is important. No one.

''Yes, well, I'll explain to the Wyndhams that you have a tremendous responsibility right now,'' she said quietly, ''and it would be best if they waited until... I can't guarantee how they'll react, but I'll do the best I can. I have to tell them that you're here, though, John. I'd be remiss in fulfilling the obligations of my position if I didn't.''

''Heaven forbid,'' he said, sarcasm ringing in his voice.

''I don't want to argue with you, John,'' Laura said wearily. ''I suggest you change your son's diaper before he becomes unhappy. I'll be in my room.''

''Hey, wait a minute. Aren't you going to help me with this diaper business?''

''No,'' she said, walking past him. ''There's no room for anyone in your life except Jeremiah, remember? Welcome to the world of fatherhood. You're on your own.''

''Well, hell,'' John said as Laura disappeared from view. He looked at Jeremiah. ''You didn't hear that, sport. Okay. Diaper time. How tough can this be?''

* * *

Twenty minutes later, John lay spread-eagle on his back on the plush area rug in front of the fireplace. Jeremiah sat next to him, beating merrily on John's chest with a wooden spoon.

False-start diapers with torn-off paper tabs were strewn around the living room, along with clothes, toys, a tube of diaper rash ointment and a box of baby wipes.

"We did it," John said, letting out a pent-up breath. "Stay dry for a week, will you, Jeremiah? I need to recuperate before I tackle that project again."

"Da, da, da," Jeremiah said, whacking John's chest with the spoon.

"That's me, if you even know what a da, da, da is," he said. "The Father of the Year. You poor kid, you've got yourself a dud here." John paused. "Well, let's give credit where it's due. You *are* wearing a dry diaper. Right? Right."

Jeremiah waved the spoon in the air, then hit John solidly on the head with the makeshift toy.

"Ow," John said. "So, okay, I don't get any points for the diaper. Satisfied?"

"John," Laura said, coming into the room, "your—oh, my stars, what happened in here? Did burglars break in and trash the place?"

John struggled to sit up, plopping Jeremiah on his lap in the process.

"Hold your tongue, woman," he said. "I'll have you know that Jeremiah is now the proud wearer of a dry diaper."

''Well, congratulations,'' Laura said with a burst of laughter.

''Thank you,'' John said, nodding decisively.

Laura's smile faded. ''John, Mitch is on the telephone and would like to speak to you.''

''Not now. I'm busy. I'll talk to him later.''

''But—''

''No, Laura,'' he said, frowning at her. ''Mitch will get into a big spiel about my being prince whoever and I don't want to hear it, think about it. Did you tell him about Jeremiah?''

''No. I spoke with your...with King Phillip and told him that you'd arrived at The Rocking C, that I'd informed you of your true identity, and that you had the Wyndham baby ring in your possession. I said you had some pressing personal business that required your full attention at the moment, and you couldn't address the issue of your heritage at the present time.''

''Oh.'' John nodded. ''Well, thank you. That ought to buy me some space.''

''Apparently everyone was gathered around while I was speaking with King Phillip,'' Laura went on, ''because I heard him relate what I said, then Mitch came on the line and asked what your pressing personal business was. I said it was up to you to tell him. So, he wants to talk to you.''

''Cripe.'' John rolled to his feet with Jeremiah in his arms. ''All right. I'll use the phone in the kitchen. Mitch better not push me about this prince stuff.''

John strode past Laura, who ducked out of the way of Jeremiah's swinging spoon. She looked at the disaster that had once been the neat-as-a-pin living room, and began to pick up the baby's clothes that were scattered across the floor.

When John returned ten minutes later, the room had been restored to a semblance of order.

"Mitch is so damn...darn...stubborn," John muttered.

"And you're not?" Laura said, raising her eyebrows.

John ignored her question. "I got Mitch to agree not to let the Wyndhams descend on me here. I think he understood that I have enough to deal with at the moment. Mitch has to get back to run the ranch, but at least he won't come home right away because the foreman he left in charge is top-notch."

Laura nodded.

"This whole thing is crazy," John went on. "How would you like to find out you're not who you thought you were for thirty years? Of course, I never really felt like a true Colton, either.... No, forget it. I'm not dwelling on it now."

Laura nodded again.

"I've got to turn that truck in to the rental office in Hope, and buy Jeremiah a decent bed and car seat."

"And clothes," Laura said. "I've stacked up what he has, John, and half of them appear to be too small. What might fit isn't going to last long because they're very threadbare."

"Dandy," John said, frowning.

"There aren't very many jars of baby food, either," Laura said. "Is he still on formula?"

"No, he just switched to regular milk."

"Well, that's a help, but you've got a major shopping expedition ahead of you. You need a playpen, too."

"What for?" John said, setting Jeremiah onto the rug in front of the hearth.

The baby dropped the spoon and crawled toward a jar of baby food that was sitting on the floor. Laura snatched up the glass jar before Jeremiah reached it.

"That's why," she said. "He has to be someplace safe so you can take a shower, or prepare a meal. Playpens have been known to save the sanity of caregivers."

"I'd better make a list of what I need before I head to town." John dragged one hand through his hair. "I'll get one of the ranch hands to follow me in so I can turn in the rented truck, then..."

Thunder boomed above the house and rain began to fall in sheets. John stared up at the ceiling.

"I don't need this," he said gruffly. "I really don't need this."

"Why don't I take care of Jeremiah while you go to town," Laura said. "It's so cold and now it's raining, and he doesn't even have shoes, or a jacket. You'll accomplish everything you need to do much faster without him along."

John smiled. "What if he needs a dry diaper while I'm gone?"

''If you can do it,'' Laura said with a shrug, ''then I can do it. How tough can it be?''

John whooped with laughter. ''That's what I said. Did you see all those little sticky tab things on the floor? I kept tearing them off before I could get them stuck on. You need an engineering degree to figure out those stupid diapers.''

Laura matched his smile. ''If all else fails, I'll use masking tape.''

''There you go,'' John said.

Their smiles disappeared slowly as they continued to look at each other. The sensual haze returned, weaving around them, igniting the embers of desire still glowing, simmering within them.

Jeremiah began to cry as a ball he'd been attempting to pick up rolled out of his grasp. Laura and John jerked to attention, then looked at the wailing baby. Laura scooped him up and patted him on the back.

''That ball is too big for you, sweetheart,'' she said. ''Your daddy will get you some new toys that are just right.'' She looked at John again. ''What bedroom are you going to set up for his nursery?''

''Jeremiah and I won't be staying in this house,'' John said.

''But where—''

''There's a furnished cabin we can use in the woods beyond the barn. Jeremiah and I will live there for now.''

''Why?''

''Because he's my son, Laura, and the only way I can learn how to be a proper father is to jump in and do it...alone.''

Chapter Four

During the following hours Laura decided she was in heaven. Jeremiah was an enchanting, happy, busy little boy, and she was having a marvelous time playing with him. His smile lit up his little face, and his laughter was like tinkling wind chimes.

At noon she set up the high chair in the kitchen and fed Jeremiah his lunch, talking to him the entire time. He opened his mouth like a hungry baby bird when the spoon approached, managing to bang noisily on the plastic tray at the same time.

Laura mastered the technique of diaper changing and mentally patted herself on the back at her expertise. She covered the crib mattress with a sheet and Jeremiah was soon snoozing away on the makeshift bed on the floor in front of the hearth.

Laura sat cross-legged on the rug next to the mattress, watching the baby sleep.

"You're beautiful and wonderful," she said softly, "and you have a magnificent father, Jeremiah. Be patient with him while he learns how to take care of you. He'll make mistakes at first, but it won't matter. What's important is that he loves you very, very much."

Laura leaned back against the sofa, her gaze still fixed on Jeremiah.

A baby like this one, she mused, was part of her rainbow wish. Oh, how she yearned to be a mother. And a wife. To have a special man in her life who loved her, would stay by her side until death parted them, her soul mate.

The image of John flitted suddenly before her mind's eye and she frowned.

What on earth was John Colton doing in her rainbow wish fantasy?

Well, it made sense, she supposed. She was tending to John's son, so her thoughts just naturally drifted to the baby's father. Yes, that was it.

She was *not* dwelling on the previous night spent with John. No. No way. This was the light of the new day, reality-check time.

John had made it crystal clear that what had happened between them was best forgotten. It was over, finished, done. He wanted nothing to do with her on a man and woman plane, because he intended to concentrate fully on raising Jeremiah.

Heavens, the man wouldn't even address the fact

that he was Prince James Wyndham of Wynborough. The heirloom ring he wore about his neck proved his identity beyond doubt. How long would it be before he was willing to acknowledge who he was and meet the members of the family he hadn't even known he had?

Laura sighed.

John was building the wall around himself and Jeremiah higher and stronger, allowing no one to come close to either of them. And now he was going to take the baby to a cabin in the woods, rather than stay in the house where he, himself, had been raised. The house where she was living for the time being.

Alone, John had said. He would learn how to be a fit and proper father to Jeremiah alone. But hadn't it occurred to John Colton that doing it all alone might lead to loneliness?

No, maybe that wasn't true in his case. Maybe he didn't need anyone special in his life. Maybe he would be just fine in that cabin with Jeremiah.

Jeremiah stirred, then stuck his thumb in his mouth and settled back into peaceful slumber.

Laura just sat there, drinking in the sight of the child who was a mirror image of his daddy. She gave up the battle and allowed Jeremiah to stake a firm and permanent hold on her heart.

And his father? she thought. All she would have of John were the memories of their night together. That was it. There was nothing more and never would be.

"So be it," she said.

Laura heard the door to the mudroom open and close, then Betty appeared in the living room moments later.

"I'm back," Betty said, "just in time to start something for supper and… There's a baby sleeping in front of the fireplace."

"There is?" Laura turned her head to smile over at the housekeeper.

Betty swept her gaze across the room, then came to stand at the end of the mattress.

"And he came with his equipment," the woman said. "What in the name of heaven is going on here?"

"John's home," Laura said.

"Oh, that explains everything," Betty said, planting her hands on her hips. "John came home, you two made whoopee and had a baby who is, oh, about a year old. I wasn't at The Triple Bar *that* long, miss. Who is that child?"

"I should let John tell you," Laura said, "but I have no idea when he'll be back from town. He had a very long shopping list when he left here because Jeremiah needs just about everything and—"

"Laura!"

"Jeremiah is John's son," Laura blurted out.

Betty stared at the sleeping baby, looked at Laura, then Jeremiah, then back at Laura.

"Well," Betty said finally, "isn't that something? John Colton is a father? That title doesn't fit him too well in my mind. Where's the mother?"

"She died," Laura said. "John just found out

about Jeremiah and has come home to raise him. Well, not exactly home, in this house. He's taking Jeremiah to a cabin in the woods beyond the barn.''

Betty nodded. ''It's a nice little place. John's a father. Good grief. Did you tell him that he's also a prince?''

''Yes,'' Laura said with a sigh, ''but he refuses to address the issue now. He said he had enough on his plate with being a new daddy.''

''The man has a point,'' Betty said. ''That baby is the spitting image of John, isn't he? Well, I'd better go open up that cabin and air it out some. I'll open the windows for a spell now that the rain has stopped, and put some food in the refrigerator. I'd better run a dust cloth over the furniture, too.''

''You don't seem surprised that John won't stay here in the house with Jeremiah.''

''Honey, nothing John Colton could do would surprise me. He's like a closed book that won't give you a peek at the pages inside.

''John has a son. Fine. John wants to tackle fatherhood on his own in the cabin in the woods. Fine. Trying to reason with John Colton once he has set his mind on something is a waste of time.''

Laura nodded.

''I sure respect what John is doing, though,'' Betty said firmly.

''What do you mean?''

''John has always been a loner, restless, edgy, on the move,'' the housekeeper said. ''A man like that could very well have turned his back on that little fella sleeping there.

"But not John Colton. There's a fine, honorable man beneath that crusty exterior. Course, I knew that all along. He's a Colton."

"He's also a Wyndham," Laura said.

"There's that, too." Betty shook her head. "Mercy sake, our John has a lot to deal with all at once, doesn't he?"

"Yes," Laura said, nodding. "Yes, he does, and he wants to deal with it all alone."

"Hmm. Do I hear the sound of sadness in your voice, Laura?"

"No, no, of course, not. That is… No, Betty, I…"

Betty laughed. "Very interesting. Well, I'm off to set things to rights in that cabin. You just tend to your boy there."

"He isn't mine," Laura said, hardly above a whisper as she gazed at Jeremiah.

Betty stared at Laura for a long moment, smiled, nodded, then spun around and headed back toward the kitchen.

"Jeremiah isn't mine," Laura said to no one, "and I *must* remember that."

John sank onto the edge of the bed and pulled off his boots, dropping each onto the floor with a thud. He flopped backward with a groan and closed his eyes.

Oh, man, he thought, he was so bone-deep tired, he'd never be able to move again. He'd just stay where he was until someone bothered to come and cart him away.

He struggled to an upright position, removed his shirt and jeans, then crawled between the cool sheets on the bed with a grateful sigh. He inhaled the aroma of fresh air and sunshine as he rolled onto his stomach and sank his head into the soft pillow.

Betty still hung the sheets on the clothesline outside, he thought foggily. Nice. That smell brought back memories of days and years long gone.

He could remember times when he'd been in some god-awful place halfway around the world, attempting to sleep on the hard ground in clothes soaked with sweat and mud, and he'd have a flash in his mind of those sweet-smelling clean sheets on his bed at the ranch.

Well, now he was home, lying on Betty's sunshine sheets, but his life was so damn complicated, it made the nights he'd slept on the ground during covert missions seem like a picnic.

Sleep. He needed sleep. He was still suffering from jet lag. On top of that he'd spent hours shopping for things for Jeremiah.

While he'd been in town he was recognized by a lot of people who greeted him with a smile, though they tried and failed to hide their surprise at his return.

He'd nodded to Lucy, the reverend's wife, and she'd sure as hell acted weird. She'd gasped, turned kind of pale, then rushed off as though something was nipping at her heels. Whatever her problem was, he'd chosen not to think about it. It wasn't important enough.

After returning to the ranch, he'd put together the new crib and a changing table, lugged all the other stuff into the cabin and found a home for everything, then finally collected his son from Laura.

Laura had fed Jeremiah his dinner, given him a bath and presented him to John in a pair of blanket sleepers and smelling like soap. The baby had, thank goodness, gone right to sleep when he'd been placed in his new crib.

Despite Laura having never changed a diaper before today, John mused sleepily, she was obviously a natural-born mother. She'd handled Jeremiah with a relaxed ease, had settled the baby on her hip the way he'd seen so many women do.

But the mighty John Colton? Hell, he felt so clumsy and inept whenever he held Jeremiah. His hands were too big and rough, and he continually worried that he would hold the baby too tightly, or not tightly enough, or—

Hell, it wasn't fair. Why did women have natural instincts about babies, while men had to learn everything from scratch? Or was it just him who was lacking, versus other men who could step in and get the job done with no problem?

"What difference does it make?" he mumbled, punching the pillow.

The fact remained that *he* was Jeremiah's father. One look at the baby was proof enough. The two of them would have to make the best of the situation. Together. Somehow.

What was he going to do?

Stay on the ranch to raise his son? Live and work on the land, a place where he'd never felt comfortable, never really fit in?

Jeremiah needed stability in his life, a home, a routine. There was a routine on The Rocking C, all right, the same monotonous work, day in, day out, on acres and acres of land that drained a man dry of strength sunup to sundown. His father and brother loved that life-style, lived and breathed it. He hated it.

John flipped onto his back and stared up at the ceiling he couldn't actually see in the darkness.

Hey, now, he thought, he didn't have to break his back working on the ranch. He was a prince, for crying out loud. Prince James Wyndham of Wynborough, wherever the hell that was.

''Cripe,'' he said aloud.

He dragged both hands down his face, then dropped his arms heavily onto the bed.

A prince. That was so bizarre, so nuts. And so true, because Laura wouldn't lie to him. He now had two sets of parents and a bunch of sisters, who were princesses, thrown in for good measure. Crazy.

Yeah, well, the fact that he, John Colton, also known as James Wyndham in royal circles, was a father wasn't too sane, either.

Poor Jeremiah. That cute, innocent little guy sure

had been stuck with a bum rap, and he didn't even know it yet.

Well, all John could do was the best he could do, one day at a time. Yeah, that was the ticket…one day at a time. Just concentrate on Jeremiah, nothing else.

He wouldn't dwell on this Prince James Wyndham of Wynborough stuff. Not now. Although it sure did explain why he'd never had a love for the land like the Coltons.

And he sure as hell wouldn't think about Laura. About how good she felt when he held her close to his heated body. About the taste of her sweet lips, the sound of her laughter, her aroma of flowers.

No, he wouldn't think about how *right* Laura had looked standing there with Jeremiah in her arms, the two of them smiling at him when he'd come through the front door.

No way. Nope. He wouldn't do a mental rerun of the fantastic night he'd spent with Laura Bishop. The talking, the sharing, the lovemaking, the—no, it was history, all of it. Over. Done. Finished.

Focus, Colton, he told himself. Focus on that baby sleeping in the other bedroom. His son.

''Right,'' he said aloud before sleep dropped over him like a heavy curtain…and he dreamed of Laura.

John sat bolt upright on the bed, reaching automatically for the gun next to him that wasn't there. He blinked, then realized that the strange noise that had awakened him was Jeremiah's wail.

He threw back the blankets, glanced quickly at the clock on the nightstand that announced it was 6:17 a.m., then made a beeline for Jeremiah's room. He barrelled inside to find Jeremiah standing up in the crib, gripping the rail and yelling at the top of his lungs.

"What? What?" John said, scooping the baby into his arms. "Oh, man, you're soaking wet. You flooded the decks, kid."

John shifted Jeremiah to hold him at arms' length, causing the baby to kick his feet in the air and laugh. John crossed the room and laid the baby on the changing table. Jeremiah rolled immediately onto his stomach, scooted up onto his hands and knees and began to crawl toward the edge of the table.

"Whoa," John said, grabbing the baby around the waist.

He replaced Jeremiah on his back, fastened the safety strap across his tummy, then realized he couldn't unzip the sleeper with the belt in place.

John stared up at the ceiling, counted to ten, then looked at Jeremiah.

"Okay, sport, we'll start over at the top." John chuckled. "Or at the bottom in this case, which is the flood zone that needs attention." He handed Jeremiah a plastic rattle. "Can you be bribed? Play with that."

Twenty minutes later, Jeremiah was dressed in a royal-blue playsuit with a smiling Big Bird on the pocket, socks and tiny blue tennis shoes. His hair was brushed and he was chewing contentedly on the rattle.

This bedroom, John thought glancing around, is a disaster area.

There was a pile of wet bedclothes on the floor, topped by the soggy sleeper. John had bumped a can of powder with his elbow, toppling it over the edge of the changing table, and talcum had flown in all directions.

The wet diaper was in a plastic trash basket, along with three dry ones that had been rendered useless when John tore off the tabs before he could stick them into place.

"Yeah, well, I'll get it shipshape later," John said, striding from the room with Jeremiah in his arms.

In the living room, John put the baby in the mesh playpen.

"There you go," he said. "You check out those spiffy new toys while I shower, then I'll fix you some breakfast. Okay?"

Jeremiah pushed himself to his feet, grabbed the top, padded edge of the playpen and cut loose with an earsplitting wail.

"No, I won't," John said, snatching up the baby. "I'll feed you, then shower. I hope you know I'm freezing to death standing here in my underwear, kid. I'm at least going to put on my jeans."

More than an hour later, John emerged from a quick shower and dressed even more quickly in jeans, socks and a flannel Western shirt. He hurried back into the living room and sighed with relief as he saw Jeremiah playing with the toys in the play-pen.

"Great stuff, huh?" John said to the baby, as he went past him on the way to the kitchen.

In the doorway of the minuscule kitchen, John stopped and shook his head.

Orange juice was dripping from the counter top in a steady, maddening rhythm. There were globs of cereal on the high chair tray, the floor, and the wall next to the high chair.

The book John had purchased titled *Parenting The Easy Way* was open on the counter to the section on "Feeding Your Toddler" and was splattered with juice, cereal and baby food peaches.

"Coffee," John muttered. "I need coffee."

A short time later, John sank onto the faded sofa in the living room with a mug of hot, strong coffee and looked at Jeremiah who was still engrossed with the toys in the playpen.

"Know something, sport?" John said. "I have new and awesome respect for the mothers of this world. They do this stuff every day and live to tell about it. They even smile a lot, Jeremiah. Can you believe that?"

"Da, da," Jeremiah said, then flung three plastic blocks out of the playpen.

"Yeah, I'm your da," John said, flipping the blocks back into the playpen. "I think I'm going to have to tear down the kitchen and rebuild it, because that cereal of yours has turned into concrete. I hate to think what it's doing to your stomach.''

Jeremiah babbled something only a baby could understand, then began to toss the toys out of the playpen, one by one. John took a sip of the hot coffee, then watched in amazement as a plastic block sailed through the air and landed squarely in the mug with a splash.

''Two points,'' John yelled, then laughed.

Jeremiah clapped his hands and smiled.

John's smile faded as he stared at his happy son.

''I'm doing the best I can, kiddo,'' he said quietly. ''But, Jeremiah? So far, I've got a knot in my gut that is telling me that my best might not be good enough.''

Laura nibbled on a piece of toast she'd slathered with homemade apple butter, realizing as she chewed and swallowed that she wasn't one bit hungry. She took a sip of hot coffee from her mug, then set it next to the plate on the table.

Betty was humming a tune as she put things into the dishwasher. The smell of cinnamon wafted through the air from the oven.

Laura sighed.

She hadn't slept well, she mused. She'd had weird, disturbing dreams that had made no sense and had caused her to wake several times in the night.

John had invaded her peaceful slumber, as had Jeremiah. There had been one dream where she'd entered a room that was filled with babies sitting on the floor. She had been searching frantically for *her* child, but had been jarred awake before she accomplished her goal. She hadn't found her baby.

"Well, I wonder how the new daddy is doing?" Betty said, bringing Laura from her thoughts.

"I'm sure he and Jeremiah are fine," Laura said, poking at the toast with one fingertip. "Jeremiah is a happy baby, not overly demanding, or fussy. He gets frustrated easily if he can't get where he wants to go, or isn't able to reach a toy, or... But if you help him a little, he's smiling again in a flash.

"Did you notice how silky his hair is, Betty? And those eyes of his. Oh, my, he's so..." Laura stopped speaking and cleared her throat. "Never mind."

Betty camouflaged a burst of laughter with a cough, then removed three pans of cinnamon rolls from the oven.

"I'll frost these once they cool a bit," she said, "then you can take a dozen down to John."

Laura stiffened in her chair. "Me? Oh, I don't think—that is, I have no idea where that cabin is that John took Jeremiah to. I'd get lost for sure and... No, it would be best if you took the rolls to John, Betty."

"Can't."

"Why not?"

"I've got eggs to gather," the housekeeper said, "a load of wash to start, a grocery list to make up. I'll tell you how to reach the cabin. You're not too busy to help me out a tad here, are you, Laura?"

"Heavens, no, but why don't *I* collect the eggs?"

Betty laughed. "Honey, those chickens don't let anyone but me gather those eggs. They don't take to strangers. They'd chase you right back out the door if you stepped foot in that coop."

"Oh."

"It's settled then," Betty said. "You take the rolls to John. You might mention to him that his parents would be thrilled to hear they have a grandson."

"John has two sets of parents," Laura said quietly.

"Well, I'm talking about Cissy and Robert Colton, the ones who raised him. John needs to get on the phone and tell them about Jeremiah."

"You want *me* to give orders to John?" Laura said, her eyes widening. "I'd rather risk gathering the eggs."

"Just *suggest* it to him," Betty said. "Course, Mitch may have already called them with the news." She paused. "Mitch needs to get back here pretty quick and tend to running this ranch."

"Yes, he does," Laura said, tracing one finger around the top of her coffee mug, "and I'll be leaving The Rocking C soon, I imagine. I've completed my assignment here."

"Guess that will be up to the princesses to decide, wouldn't you say?"

"Well, yes. I work for them."

"Yep. Well, finish your coffee and go get your jacket. I'll have these rolls frosted and ready to be delivered to John by then. You can tell him I'll have groceries for him late this afternoon.''

Laura got to her feet and carried her mug and plate to the sink.

''Just leave those things on the counter,'' Betty said. ''I want John to have these rolls while they're still warm. He loves these things, and it's been far too long since he's been home to have some.''

''I'll get my jacket.''

In her room, Laura retrieved her jacket from the closet, put it on, then sank onto the edge of the bed.

She did not, she thought dismally, want to deliver those cinnamon rolls to John Colton. She was not doing well at all, tucking away the memories of her night with John, not reliving those glorious hours spent with him, not recalling every vivid, meaningful and sensuous detail.

The mere thought of John, the briefest image of him in her mind's eye, threw her off-kilter, caused her heart to race and heat to swirl throughout her. She felt too vulnerable, too exposed somehow, to go blissfully knocking on his door with goodies in tow.

Oh, John Colton was a dangerous man. He was staking some sort of eerie claim on her, weaving a spell over her, making it impossible to think clearly.

And Jeremiah? As far as John's son was concerned, she was a goner. That adorable baby had captured her heart, no doubt about it.

Laura sighed and got to her feet.

She had no choice but to go to the cabin in the woods. To refuse Betty's request to complete the errand would reveal far more than she was prepared to explain.

So, okay. She'd go. She could handle this. She'd shove the dumb rolls at John, then hightail it out of there. Fine. She was under control.

Then why, she thought, as she started toward the bedroom door, did she feel like Little Red Riding Hood about to go calling on the Big Bad Wolf?

Chapter Five

Laura stomped across the pasture behind the barn, then entered the wooded area beyond. Her tennis shoes became immediately soaked from the underbrush that was still cold and wet from the rain the previous day.

Her now damp, chilly feet did nothing to improve her rapidly deteriorating mood, nor did the wicker basket she carried that made her feel even more ridiculously like Little Red Riding Hood.

She was the social secretary for the Royal Princesses of Wynborough, she mentally fumed, not a cinnamon roll delivery person.

"Oh, Laura, shut up," she said aloud. "You sound like a snob."

Not only that, she thought with a sigh, she wasn't

fooling herself one iota. She didn't mind helping Betty, would have gladly shopped for groceries, washed the kitchen floor, even taken on the crabby chickens. She would have volunteered happily for any chore other than delivering the damnable rolls to John Colton.

John Colton. Prince James Wyndham of Wynborough.

John did not fit the fairy-tale image of a prince, that was for sure. Well, maybe that wasn't quite fair. He *had* rescued her from the villainous Pete in Jake's Saloon. That was rather…well, princely of John, if there was such a word.

And then, of course, there was the fairy-tale magic of their night together, beginning with heartfelt sharing and caring, and ending with lovemaking so incredibly beautiful, it defied description. Yes, John had been her magical prince for one night stolen out of time…and reality.

Reality.

Laura sighed again and slowed her step as a glimpse of the cabin came into view among the tall trees.

She had to stay firmly grounded in reality when she saw John *and* Jeremiah. John was centered on raising his son, wanted nothing, nor anyone else, intruding on his mission. Jeremiah was the son in question, and belonged solely to his father. The end.

"Got that, Ms. Bishop?" she said aloud.

Laura stopped as she emerged from the woods to the clearing surrounding the red brick cabin.

Oh, how charming, she thought. It was picture-perfect cute. The brick cabin had white trim, complete with shutters banking the windows, and smoke curling from the chimney like a welcoming sign that someone was home and a warming fire was beckoning in the hearth.

Laura drew a steadying breath, then marched to the white front door and rapped sharply. She frowned as she leaned closer and heard Jeremiah wailing inside. She knocked again, louder.

"All right. All right," she heard John yell. "I'm coming. Keep your pants on."

He could have gone all day without saying *that,* Laura thought, rolling her eyes heavenward. A lot more than pants had been flung aside when she and John had—

The door was whipped open, bringing Laura back to attention. John stood towering over her, a screaming Jeremiah tucked under one arm like a football, a dripping sponge in John's other hand.

"Gracious," Laura said, raising her voice to be heard above Jeremiah. "What on earth are you doing to that poor child?"

"I'm not washing *him,*" John said, glaring at her. "I'm attempting to get cereal off the kitchen wall, but he keeps getting in the way."

"Oh," Laura said, nodding slowly. "I see." She paused. "No, I don't. How did the cereal get on the wall?"

"Jeremiah kept whacking the spoon when I... Are you coming in or what?"

"No, no, my feet are wet. I'm just delivering these cinnamon rolls to you from Betty. They're still warm, just the way you like them. She'll have groceries for you this afternoon, and she suggested you call your parents and tell them about Jeremiah, because they'd be thrilled to hear they have a grandson."

Laura took a gulp of much-needed air.

"Unless you figure that Mitch already told them," she finished in a rush. "There. Here." She held out the basket toward John.

"My hands are full," John said. "Come on in."

"But my feet…"

"The place is a wreck anyway. You're not going to hurt it." John stepped back. "Hurry up. The heat is getting out through the door."

Laura stepped into the cabin and swept her gaze over the small living room as John closed the door.

"Oh, it's lovely," she said. "Homey, cozy, very nice." She laughed. "And decorated with toys."

"Yeah, well, Jeremiah got fed up with being in the playpen after he tossed everything out. I put the toys back in three times, but he was determined to escape. Take him for a second, would you?"

Laura set the basket on the sofa, then retrieved Jeremiah from his horizontal position under John's arm. She held the baby close.

"Hi, sweetheart," she said to a still-screaming Jeremiah. "You're certainly unhappy at the moment. Hush, hush, don't cry."

Jeremiah drew a wobbly breath, stuck his thumb

in his mouth and laid his head on Laura's shoulder. She rubbed his back in a circling motion.

"Well, cripe," John said, frowning. "How did you do that? I tried everything I could think of to get him to stop crying, but..." He sighed and shook his head. "I'm such a dud at this father bit. I haven't done more than one or two things right so far, if that many."

"You've just begun, John," Laura said. "Don't be so hard on yourself. You can't be expected to do everything perfectly right off the bat." She glanced at Jeremiah, then looked at John again. "He's asleep. He apparently still takes a morning nap. He was tired, that's all."

"Well, how was I supposed to know that?" John said forcefully.

"Shh. You'll wake him up. Where's his crib?"

"I had the guys take the furniture out of one of the bedrooms," John said, jerking his head to the left. "I put Jeremiah's crib and stuff in there."

"Okay. I'll go settle him in," Laura said, starting forward.

John blocked her way, and she looked up at him questioningly.

"I need to talk to you after you put Jeremiah to bed. Okay?" John said quietly. "Don't run off while I'm attacking the kitchen wall."

"Yes, all right. Excuse me."

John moved out of Laura's way, then watched her disappear down the short hallway and into Jeremiah's bedroom. He spun around and strode back toward the kitchen.

"Why didn't he say he was tired?" he muttered. "I'm supposed to be a mind reader here? Poor little kid was wiped out and I didn't even know it. Lousy father. Crummy, rotten, lousy father."

In the bedroom, Laura eased Jeremiah from her shoulder and placed him on his back in the crib. He stirred, then stilled, his little hands flung out on either side of his head. She untied the tennis shoes, removed them, then smiled as she looked at the tiny shoes.

After placing the tennies on the end of the changing table, Laura saw a large trash bag filled with bedclothes and topped by an obviously wet blanket sleeper. She laughed softly, then returned to the crib to gaze at the sleeping baby.

"So precious," she whispered. "Oh, Jeremiah, I'm so glad to see you again. You've stolen my heart, little one, you truly have."

And his father? she thought, shifting her gaze to the doorway.

Don't do it, Laura, she told herself. She mustn't start thinking about John Colton as anything other than Jeremiah's father. Oh, and, yes, as the Prince of Wynborough. They were both titles, roles, that had absolutely nothing to do with her.

Laura looked at Jeremiah for another long moment, then turned and left the room.

* * *

In the kitchen, Laura saw that John had placed the plate of cinnamon rolls in the center of the small table.

"Coffee?" he said, holding up the pot.

"Well...yes, all right," Laura said, sitting down in one of the chairs. "Thank you."

John carried two mugs to the table, then retraced his steps to deposit a spoon, a quart of milk and a five-pound bag of sugar in front of Laura.

"There," he said, sitting down opposite her. "Here," he added, handing her a napkin from a stack near his elbow. "Help yourself to Betty's cinnamon rolls. They're the best in the world, and I should know, because I've sampled my share around the globe."

Laura pulled one of the rolls free, took a bite, then set it on the napkin. John polished off a roll and reached for another.

"Mmm," Laura said. "You're right. They're delicious." She paused. "You've done a great deal of traveling in your life, haven't you?"

John nodded, then took a sip of the hot coffee.

"Do you think it will be difficult," Laura said, "for you to stay in one place to raise Jeremiah?"

John shrugged.

"Have you given any thought at all to the incredible fact that you're Prince James Wyndham of Wynborough?"

John shook his head.

"Gosh, John," Laura said, frowning, "don't talk so much. You're hardly giving me a chance to say anything. You were the one who said you wished to speak with me. So…speak, for heaven's sake.''

''Yeah, well, the subject matter isn't my future plans for Jeremiah, nor this crazy business about me being a prince,'' he said. ''What's on my mind is the present, this very moment.''

''And?'' Laura said, raising her eyebrows.

John sighed. ''Laura, I need help with Jeremiah. It's not fair to him for me to be practicing being a father, especially since I'm screwing everything up and he's paying the price for what I don't know.''

''But you said you wanted to learn the ropes of fatherhood alone, John.''

''I was wrong, okay? I admit that,'' he said, volume on high. ''I didn't know that being a father was so damn complicated.''

''You don't have to yell,'' Laura yelled.

John raised both hands. ''I'm sorry. Laura, look, I'm afraid I'll harm Jeremiah in some way, because of my lack of knowledge. I can't allow that to happen. I need to be taught what to do for him, not just wing it. Please. I'm asking for your help.''

Funny little fingers of warmth tiptoed around Laura's heart as she stared at John.

Oh, my stars, she thought, how very difficult it must be for John to do this. His masculine pride and self-esteem must be in shreds, but he was putting Jeremiah's needs first. John Colton was such an incredible man, a wonderful father, a—

''Laura?''

''Oh. Well, what did you have in mind?''

"You're staying on The Rocking C, aren't you?" he said.

"For now," she said, nodding. "Until the princesses tell me otherwise. Truth be known, I'm not certain that I'll still have a job with the royal family, because the princesses are married, scattered here and there. They may no longer need a social secretary."

"So, you're at the ranch until you get other orders, or whatever." John dragged one hand through his hair. "Maybe you could spend the days here, in the cabin with me and Jeremiah.

"I could learn what to do for him by watching you, taking instructions from you. Jeremiah deserves better than how I'm handling him on my own. Will you do it?"

No! Laura's mind yelled. Merciful saints, no.

Spend hours and hours tending to a baby who had already claimed her heart? A baby she would eventually have to walk away from, never to see again?

Spend hours and hours with a man who evoked desire within her with a mere look, smile, the sound of his voice, the rumble of his laughter?

A magnificent man she had spent the most glorious night of her life with, the memories of which refused to stay put away where they belonged? A dangerous man, who might very well cause her to fall in love with him before she was forced to leave him?

No, absolutely not.

She'd have to be certifiably insane to agree to John's request.

"Laura?" John said quietly.

"Yes," she said, looking directly into his eyes. "I'll...I'll help you with Jeremiah, John."

Oh, her poor parents, she thought rather hysterically. Their youngest daughter was a fruitcake. She was crazy, completely nuts. She was setting herself up for potential heartache and—

Laura jerked in surprise as John reached around the bulky bag of sugar and covered her hand with his on top of the table.

"Thank you," he said, meeting her gaze. "My son thanks you, too, although he doesn't realize it. You're a very special woman, Laura. I meant what I said in that note I wrote you. I sincerely hope you find your rainbow of happiness, because you deserve to have it."

Do not cry, Laura Bishop, she ordered herself frantically. She could feel the achy sensation in her throat, the stinging at the back of her eyes.

She could deal with John much easier when he was grumpy and hollering his head off. But when he was sweet, tender, borderline romantic and sentimental? Her bones were dissolving and she was a breath away from bursting into tears. The man just didn't play fair.

Ah, man, John thought, what had he done? Laura looked as though she was about to cry. What had he said to upset her like this?

He sure was on a crummy roll. He couldn't take

proper care of his own baby son, and now he'd said, or done, something to bring this special, rare and wonderful woman close to tears.

"Hey," he said, releasing Laura's hand and getting to his feet. "Laura?"

He came around the table, drew her up and into his embrace, and held her close.

"Talk to me," he said. "I've obviously done something wrong."

"No." Laura sniffled. "No, you didn't."

"You're speaking to my shirt. Look at me."

Laura lifted her head slowly to meet his gaze. He nearly groaned aloud when he saw the tears shimmering in her lovely, big green eyes.

"Ah, Laura, I'm sorry," he said. "I don't know what I did, but I'm sorry for...whatever it was."

"No, no, please don't apologize, because you'll make me feel even more foolish than I already do. It's just that what you said about my finding my rainbow... It was so-o-o sweet."

"Ah-h-h," he said, smiling at her. "Those tears are the one hundred percent feminine kind that men won't live long enough to understand. Right?"

"Yes, that's right," she said, managing to produce a small smile.

John's smile faded as he became acutely aware of the heat beginning to coil low in his body where Laura was nestled so enticingly against him.

Let her go, Colton, he ordered himself. *Drop your arms, take a step backward and, damn it, let her go.*

He didn't move.

He *couldn't* move. Hell, he could hardly breathe, and his heart was beating so wildly, he could hear the echo of it in his ears.

He hadn't intended to touch Laura, to hold her, but now that he was… Ah, hell.

John lowered his head and claimed Laura's lips in a searing kiss.

The kiss was fire, igniting the glowing embers of desire still within them into licking flames of passion that consumed them instantly. Their tongues met, tasting of sweet cinnamon rolls and coffee, stroking, dueling, dancing.

Memories of their lovemaking swept over them in a rush, heightening their passion even more.

John raised his head a fraction of an inch to draw a rough breath, then claimed Laura's lips again. She leaned into him, returning the kiss in total abandon.

Colton, John's mind roared, *get a grip.*

He broke the kiss, raised his hands to Laura's shoulders and eased her away from his aroused body.

"No," he said, his voice raspy.

Laura blinked, shook her head slightly, and took a deep, wobbly breath.

"No?" she said.

John stepped backward and Laura sank onto her chair, her trembling legs refusing to hold her for another second.

"I didn't mean for that to happen," John said, "and it won't be repeated. I asked you to help me with Jeremiah. I don't want you to think that request means I intend to hustle you into bed. I won't touch you again, Laura.''

But she wanted to be hustled into John's bed, Laura thought frantically. She wanted to make exquisite love with him for hours and hours, soar to that wondrous place with him, feel so womanly, and special, and beautiful.

I won't touch you again, Laura.

John's words beat against Laura's heart and mind, and a chill swept through her, causing her to shiver.

Despite the intensity of the kisses they'd just shared, John didn't want her, desire her, as she did him. He was making that very clear. And it hurt. Dear heaven, how it hurt.

Grow up, Laura, she admonished herself. John was worldly and sophisticated enough to have shoved the memories of their night together into some dusty corner of his mind, far, far away from his heart. Well, she could—would—do the same. Somehow.

''Yes, fine,'' she said, shifting in her chair to pick up her coffee mug. ''I'm just the baby-sitter, the person who will teach you how to care for your son.''

''Yeah,'' John said, sitting down opposite her.

That was the way it had to be, he told himself. No doubt about it. He knew that. He didn't have room in his life for anyone but Jeremiah. Damn it, he knew that.

Besides, he had absolutely no experience where serious, long-term relationships were concerned.

He'd always been on the move, involving himself with women who understood he wouldn't be around forever.

He didn't even know if he was capable of making a lifelong commitment to a woman. He just wasn't in Laura's league. She was a hearth-and-home, till-death-do-us-part kind of lady who deserved better than him. He knew that.

Then why did he feel so empty? So alone?

"Could you stay here in the cabin now?" he said, staring into his mug. "I need to go up to the house and do a load of wash. Jeremiah soaked his bed, big time."

"Yes, I'm free now," Laura said quietly.

"Good. That's good. Thanks."

John got to his feet and strode from the room. A few minutes later, Laura heard the front door close behind him. She plunked her elbow on the table, rested her chin in her hand and sighed.

"Laura Bishop," she said dismally, "if you fall in love with that man, if John and Jeremiah become your rainbow wish, I'll never speak to you again."

Chapter Six

John sat in the butter-soft leather chair behind the desk in the den in the ranch house, the telephone receiver cradled between his head and shoulder.

"So that's it, Mom," he said. "That brings you up to speed on what's going on."

"Well, you certainly are full of news, John," Cissy Colton said. "Your father and I will want pictures of Jeremiah. I'm sure there's a camera round there someplace." She paused. "A grandson. I admit it's all a bit shocking, but oh, my, I'm so thrilled. I can hardly wait to get my hands on that baby."

John chuckled. "I could use your experienced hands, that's for sure. So far, I haven't done a bang-up job of being a father."

"Give it time. You'll get the hang of it. Besides, you said that Laura Bishop is helping you out."

"Yes," John said quietly. "Yes, she is. She's a natural-born mother, just senses, knows, what Jeremiah needs. Laura is a very special woman, very..." He cleared his throat. "Anyway, Laura is pitching in for now."

"I see," Cissy said. "How nice for you that she's such a *special* woman."

"Don't make a big deal out of it, Mom. I just meant that Jeremiah will benefit from Laura's expertise."

"Yes, of course. John, we need to discuss what you've learned about your true identity."

"No," he said gruffly. "I'm not thinking about that right now. I have parents...you and Dad. I'm John Colton. End of story."

"You're also Prince James Wyndham of Wynborough," Cissy said. "My gracious, that's a lot to take in all at once, isn't it? My son, a prince."

"Mom, all I'm dealing with at the present time is Jeremiah."

"I understand your attitude, John. Becoming an instant father is rather daunting. But will you please think about something else. For me?"

"What is it?"

"My darling, all these years your biological parents thought you were dead, that you were killed by whoever kidnapped you as an infant.

"Oh, John, can't you understand what those people must be feeling? Their son is alive. Can't you imagine the joy, the sense of a miracle having taken place, that must be consuming them?''

''I...''

''John, you will always be my son. Nothing will ever change that in my heart. But there is another set of parents who need to see you in order to be able to truly believe that you're alive and well.

''The pain and loss they have suffered all these years is over. Their son is alive, John. Don't make them wait too long to meet you. Please.''

John sighed and ran the fingertips of one hand over his forehead where a headache was beginning to throb.

''I didn't think about all that,'' he said. ''I simply decided I had enough on my plate because of Jeremiah.''

''I realize that,'' Cissy said, ''but there are others involved in this besides just you.''

''Yes, ma'am,'' John said, smiling. ''I hear you talking, ma'am.''

''Good. I know you'll do the right thing, John, and soon.''

John rolled his eyes heavenward. ''Yes, Mother.''

''Fine. Kiss Jeremiah for me, and I'll talk to you in a few days. And, John? Your father and I love you very much. And we agree your having two sets of parents should be a bonus, not a burden, for you.''

''Oh, yeah? What about the fact that I'm a prince, for crying out loud?''

"Well, you were never content being a rancher. Who knows? You just might enjoy being a prince."

"Ah, hell," John said, shaking his head.

"Don't swear. I don't want to hear that kind of language coming from Jeremiah. Well, I must go. Owning a bed-and-breakfast doesn't make for idle hours.

"Your father and I will come to the ranch to see you and your son as soon as we can make arrangements for someone to step in for us here for a bit. Goodbye for now."

"'Bye, Mom. Tell Dad I said hello."

John replaced the telephone receiver, then leaned his head back and stared at the ceiling. He took a deep breath and exhaled slowly, puffing out his cheeks.

Man, oh, man, he thought, his life was suddenly so complicated, so filled with…with people.

For as long as he could remember he'd been a loner, standing just on the edge, the outsider looking in.

Yes, he loved his brother, Mitch, and his parents, Cissy and Robert. He truly did. But he'd never fit in, couldn't comprehend, nor embrace, their devotion to the land, the hours and hours of labor that never produced a sense of completion.

As a government agent, a mercenary of sorts, he'd found a sense of purpose, a discipline he took to as naturally as breathing. Each assignment he was given had a beginning and an end. He did what needed to be done, then it was over. Finished. Done.

And he did it alone.

His family had accepted him as he was, never pushed, never pressured him. Whenever he returned home to The Rocking C, he was welcomed with open arms and loving hearts. Whether it had been two months or two years since he had been home, the love showered on him was unconditional, warm and real.

But now?

Hell, he was surrounded by people, all of whom wanted, needed, something from him.

There was another set of parents who, he now realized from what his mother had said, were eager to see him, to get to know him, to be able to lay to rest the years of pain and heartache caused by believing that he was dead.

There were sisters, too, the Royal Princesses of Wynborough, who wished to meet the brother they had never known. How did a man sit down and have a conversation with a bunch of highfalutin' princesses, for cripe sake?

There was Jeremiah, his son, an innocent, helpless baby, who had no one but him, John Colton, to raise him, to provide a home for him, a sense of belonging.

He wanted for Jeremiah what he'd never been able to obtain for himself...a sense of belonging, roots, inner peace and contentment with who he was and where he lived.

And there was Laura.

John jerked forward in the chair.

No. Whoa. Wait a minute. Laura wasn't in this picture. Yes, okay, she was very special and he...he cared for her. Their night together meant a great deal to him. But while all the other new people in his life were permanent fixtures, wouldn't disappear, Laura would soon be gone. She was here temporarily, waiting to find out what plans the Wyndhams had for her.

He and Jeremiah would be alone again, just the two of them, staring at the sea of new faces belonging to people declaring themselves to be the family he hadn't even known existed.

John raked both hands through his hair.

What a dreary scenario he was painting in his mind. Laura was the one person he felt really connected to, the one he could talk to, holding nothing back.

But Laura would be gone.

He'd never again see her smile, hear her laughter, watch her beautiful green eyes become smoky with desire for him. *Him.*

He wouldn't be able to hold her in his arms, pull her close, drink in the taste and aroma of her.

Soon, at any moment, he supposed, Laura could receive word that she was to return to Wynborough and resume her duties there. Or she might be informed that her services were no longer needed and she'd explore new avenues for her future.

Her future. She wanted to find her rainbow of happiness, to be a wife and mother. That was her secret wish that she'd shared with him during the magical night they'd spent together.

Yeah, well, Laura didn't have impossible dreams. There was a man out there somewhere who would realize how special she was, love her the way she deserved to be loved, give her a slew of babies to nurture.

He frowned. That picture was *not* appealing to him one iota. Some faceless guy touching Laura? Kissing her? Making love to her? Some macho jerk crowing about his virility as Laura grew big with his child?

"No way," John said, lunging to his feet. "I'll shoot him if he lays one hand on her."

Great, he thought, shaking his head in self-disgust. He was slipping over the edge. He had so much coming at him from all directions that he was on the verge of totally losing it.

He should grab Jeremiah and leave, just head out for parts unknown and see where they ended up.

John began to pace the large room.

No, he couldn't do that. He'd been running all his life, looking for something he'd never found. It was time to stop that futile search and create a home, a stable and serene existence for his son. Jeremiah deserved and needed that. He'd do it for his boy. Somehow.

Jeremiah also had the right to bask in the love that would be forthcoming from Mitch, Cissy and Robert. Hell, Jeremiah had *two* sets of grandparents and a bunch of aunts, for crying out loud. His son had a huge family, waiting to welcome him into the fold.

So many people, John thought, continuing his trek around the room. Crowding him. Pressing in on him. Wanting a part of him. Didn't they realize he had nothing to offer them? That he'd never be what they expected him to be?

He stopped by a globe that was mounted on a wooden stand. He spun the ball until it was a blur of colors, then he stopped it with a smack of his hand.

Wynborough. In all his travels, he'd never even heard of the place.

He lifted his hand and stared at the globe, his heart suddenly beating in a wild tempo as he saw what was beneath his palm.

There it was, he thought incredulously. Wynborough. It was a small island in the North Atlantic. That was where he'd been born as James Wyndham. Proud and happy young parents had gazed at their miracle, their son, rejoicing in his birth.

And then?

Their lives had been shattered when that baby had been kidnapped. There, in Wynborough, tears had been shed as heartache so intense it defied description had torn at those parents when they came to believe that their baby was dead.

He'd only known Jeremiah for a handful of hours, but the thought of someone taking his son away, ripping him out of his life, was chilling, would be more than he could bear.

But his biological parents had lived that hideous nightmare for all these years, their pain probably dulling but never disappearing totally from their hearts, minds and souls.

And now?

He had the power, by simply being alive, to erase the dark cloud of sorrow and despair that had hung over those people's heads for so very, very long.

And the very thought of being pulled into that ecstatic family was causing a cold fist to tighten in his gut. The image in his mind's eye was of smothering arms reaching for him, wanting to hold him fast in a world across the sea that he knew nothing about.

He'd feel like a bug trapped under a microscope, being peered at, examined, as determinations were made as to whether or not he was worthy of his title. Prince. Son. Brother.

He'd failed miserably in his role of being a true Colton. There was no way in hell he would ever measure up to the lofty levels of being a Wyndham.

"Ah, man," John said, pressing the heels of his hands against his eyes, "why don't they all just go away and leave me alone? Let me get on with my life with Jeremiah and Laura and..."

He dropped his hands and stiffened.

Jeremiah *and* Laura?

"Okay, that's it," he said, spinning around. "I'm losing my mind."

"That's no bulletin," Betty said from the doorway of the den.

John chuckled despite the raging turmoil in his beleaguered mind.

"Hello, Betty," he said, smiling. "Thanks for the cinnamon rolls. Having them for breakfast was just like old times."

Betty leaned one shoulder against the doorjamb. "But everything else in your life is new and different, isn't it, John?"

"You can say that again. I'm in deep, deep trouble here."

"Oh, not necessarily," she said. "Changes can be unsettling, but they aren't automatically bad. You've got to give yourself some time to adjust, for things to calm down a bit." She paused. "Where's that darling baby of yours?"

"Laura is with him at the cabin. I came up to do a load of wash and to call my folks."

Betty nodded. "Good. I'm glad you phoned them. I know without asking that your parents were thrilled to learn they have a grandson."

"Yes. They're...they're remarkable people, my parents," he said quietly. "They've always accepted me as I am, even though I'm sure I was a disappointment to them."

Betty pushed herself away from the doorjamb and crossed the room to stand in front of John.

"What's this nonsense you're spouting?" she said, planting her hands on her hips.

"Come on, Betty," John said, frowning. "I'm not completely stupid. A true Colton would have been dedicated to the land, this ranch, the life-style here. I split the moment I was old enough to go.''

"So? Your folks never expected you to be a carbon copy of Robert or Mitch just because they adopted you and made you a Colton. They respected your right to be true to yourself, who you are.''

"Oh, yeah?'' he said, his voice rising. "And just who in the hell am I, Betty? There's a whole slew of people on some island in the North Atlantic who are now expecting me to behave like a prince.

"What will my first assignment be? Get on my white horse and ride out to find Sleeping Beauty so I can kiss her awake?''

"Now that,'' Betty said laughing, "was funny.''

"There's nothing humorous about this entire mess,'' he said gruffly. "The only patch of sunshine in my life right now is Jeremiah and... Forget it.''

"And Laura?'' Betty said, raising her eyebrows.

"I didn't say that. I have to go fold my wash.''

"You do that,'' Betty said as John moved around her. "Is Laura coming back up to the house?''

John stopped in the doorway, his back to her. "No, Laura is going to be spending time at the cabin, helping me out with Jeremiah, teaching me how to tend to him.''

"Ah,'' Betty said.

John turned and glared at her. "What's that supposed to mean? That...that 'ah?'''

"Nothing. Nothing at all.'' Betty flapped her hands at him. "Go get your wash out of my way. I have laundry to do, too.''

"Mmm," he said, then strode away.

"This is getting better by the minute," Betty said, laughing softly.

Laura sat at the kitchen table, humming as she chopped carrots on a wooden cutting board, then dropped them into a soup pot she'd discovered in a bottom cupboard.

She'd finished cleaning the cereal-splattered kitchen, then began to explore. She'd found a package of beef in the freezer, defrosted it in the small microwave oven, then cut it into cubes and browned them in a frying pan with some onions.

The enticing aroma of the meat and onions still lingered in the air as she prepared the vegetables for the stew she was creating.

The front door of the cabin opened and closed, then moments later John appeared in the kitchen carrying a stack of clean, folded laundry.

"Hi," Laura said, smiling. "I'm making stew for dinner tonight. I hope that's all right."

"Well, sure, that's great," John said, smiling slightly, "but I don't expect you to cook."

"Do *you* know how to cook?"

John chuckled. "No."

"That settles it then. Besides, this is fun. I haven't prepared a meal in the five years I've worked for the Wyndhams. There's a chef on staff at the palace in Wynborough."

"They live in a palace?" John said, his voice rising. "An honest-to-goodness palace?"

Laura shrugged. "They are the royal family, you know. Granted, it's an historic structure, has been there forever, but it's very homey and comfortable."

"Hmm. Is Jeremiah still asleep?"

"Yes, he's taking a really long nap. Of course, he could be off his routine due to the upheaval he's been through. His life, as he's known it, has totally changed."

"There's a lot of that going around." John set the laundry on one of the chairs, then sat down opposite Laura. "Any cinnamon rolls left?"

"Nope," she said, laughing. "I ate them. Those yummy things are addictive."

"Yep, they are. Mitch and I used to polish off a pan each when Betty baked them." John drummed his fingers on the table in a restless, edgy rhythm. "I...um...I called my folks while I was up at the house. There's no telephone in this cabin, in case you haven't noticed. Will that be a problem if the Wyndhams are trying to reach you?"

"No. I can always return their call. Back up to the part where you called your parents."

"I only spoke with my mother," John said, still tapping the table. "My dad was busy somewhere. They own a bed-and-breakfast in Washington State. The San Juan Islands, actually. They retired, got bored, and took on a brand-new endeavor."

"Good for them."

"Yeah, they like it fine, I guess. Sure is different from ranching, but it seems to suit them."

"People can change their life-styles and still be

contented, John," Laura said, glancing up at him before attacking another carrot.

"Well, I'm going to find out if I'm one of those people, aren't I?"

Laura smiled. "Yes, you certainly are." She paused. "What did your mother say about Jeremiah?"

"She was very excited. She wants pictures of him and the whole nine yards."

"Did you talk about the Wyndhams and how you feel about being one of them?"

John sighed. "Yeah. My mom was cool, steady, didn't feel threatened because I suddenly have this whole new family.

"She said I'd always be her son, but she could certainly understand that my biological parents want—need—to meet me, to see for themselves that I'm really alive after all those years of believing I was dead."

Laura nodded.

"But I feel so damn pressured, pushed to the wall. What would I say to those people? Hey, how's life in the royal fast lane?

"They're going to expect so much from me, and I have nothing to give them. They're strangers. They're—hell, listen to me. I get around you and I turn into a motormouth. I don't talk this much. Ever."

Laura's hands stilled and she looked directly into John's eyes.

"Except to me," she said softly. "Everyone

needs someone they can share their thoughts with, John. We've been doing that with each other from the moment we met. There's nothing wrong with that.''

"No, I guess there isn't.'' John flattened his hands on the top of the table and continued to meet Laura's gaze. "There's nothing *wrong* about anything we've shared.''

A flutter of heat stirred in Laura's body as instant images of them making love flitted across her mental vision.

She tore her gaze from John's and picked up a potato.

"Laura,'' John said, his voice slightly raspy, "when I walked back here from the house, I could feel this mess I'm in begin to slide off my shoulders, like dropping a heavy burden.

"I came into the cabin and shut the door, closed it against the Wyndhams and their needs. Inside these walls it's just me, Jeremiah and...and you.''

Laura's head snapped up. "John, don't.''

"It's true. No one can come through that door unless I allow them to.''

"The Wyndhams aren't going to go away,'' she said. "You can't play ostrich, pretend they're not out there waiting for you. Is that the lesson you want to teach your son? When the going gets tough, run and hide?''

A flash of anger crossed John's face, then disappeared in the next instant.

"No," he said. "That's not what I want to teach Jeremiah."

"Fine. Good." Laura began to peel the potato. "Jeremiah will learn to face things head-on, and hopefully know how to be true to himself."

"That's quite a menu."

"Well, it's all very important," she said, cubing the potato. "A man—a woman, too, of course—should know what he wants, needs."

"I see," John said slowly. "That's very important, huh?"

"It certainly is," she said decisively.

John leaned forward and snagged one of Laura's wrists.

"Okay," he said. "I want, need, to make love with you, Laura Bishop."

Laura dropped the knife onto the pile of potato cubes and stared at John with wide eyes.

"What?" she said.

"You heard me. You're the one who said a man should be true to himself, to his wants and needs. I want you, Laura."

"But…"

"You also said a woman should do the same thing. So? Do you want me, too? Do you, Laura?"

"Stop it," she said, her voice trembling. "We agreed that we'd had one glorious night together, but it was over. You can't just suddenly change the rules."

"Why not? Damn it, Laura, what happens inside this cabin has nothing to do with what's waiting beyond the door. We wouldn't be hurting anyone by—''

''Having an affair?'' she said, yanking her arm free of his hold. ''A tacky little fling? Play house? Be mommy, daddy and baby? No, thank you, Mr. Colton. Or should I call you Prince James? Whoever you are, you're despicable.''

John sank back in his chair and frowned. ''And you're mad as hell.''

''You've got that straight, buster,'' she said with an indignant little sniff. ''I do not—repeat, *do not*—engage in meaningless romps in the hay.''

John got to his feet, planted his hands on the table and leaned forward to speak close to Laura's lips.

''I wasn't implying that you did,'' he said, his voice very low, very rumbly and very, very male. ''What you and I shared in that motel was special, rare, beautiful.

''No, we don't have a chance in hell of a future together because we come from different worlds. But we do have the now. It's here, it's ours.'' He brushed his lips over hers. ''Think about it,'' he said before picking up the laundry from the chair and striding out of the kitchen.

Chapter Seven

To Laura's heartfelt relief, John returned to the kitchen carrying a babbling Jeremiah.

"Well, hello, sweet boy," Laura said, smiling. "I was beginning to think you were going to sleep the day away. I bet you're ready for a snack."

"Snack?" John said.

"Sure," she said. "Put him in the high chair and give him a couple of crackers and some bite-size cheese cubes. He can have apple juice in that cup with the lid and spout thing."

"Got it," John said. "Okay, sport, your dad is going to fix you a gourmet snack. I'll have you know, Laura, that I changed his diaper on the first shot."

"You're a pro," Laura said, laughing.

Jeremiah clapped his hands right on cue and John's laughter mingled with Laura's.

After Jeremiah had devoured his snack and Laura had put the pot of stew on the stove to simmer, the trio went into the living room. They sat on the floor in front of the warming fire in the hearth and played with Jeremiah.

Laura and John built towers of blocks that Jeremiah toppled over with squeals of delight. They rolled a ball back and forth among them, taught the baby how to play patty-cake, entertained him with mouse and rabbit hand puppets, then John settled onto the sofa with Jeremiah on his lap and read him the story of Snow White.

"This isn't a good book to read to a kid," John said to Laura. "This gal is living with seven guys."

Laura dissolved in a fit of laughter, and one by one, she stored the memories safely away in the treasure chest in her heart.

After Laura straightened up the kitchen once lunch was over, she walked into the living room, then stopped, hardly breathing, as she drank in the sight before her.

John was stretched out on the sofa asleep with a snoozing Jeremiah tummy-down on his daddy's chest, his little head tucked beneath John's chin. One of John's large hands was spread across the baby's back. The storybook had slid unnoticed to the floor.

Tears filled Laura's eyes and she pressed trembling fingertips to her lips.

Oh, look at them, she thought. They were so beautiful, so perfect. And each of them was staking a claim on her heart.

She had no defenses left, was succumbing to emotions so powerful they were consuming her, rendering her incapable of keeping a firm hold on reality.

Jeremiah was the child she'd yearned for, the baby she wanted to love and nurture, watch as he grew into a wonderful man ready to face the challenges of his future.

And John? Slowly but surely, she was losing the battle to keep her growing feelings for him in check. Inch by emotional inch, she was falling in love with John Colton...Prince James Wyndham of Wynborough.

Oh, how foolish she was. Her lack of experience and sophistication was going to cause her the greatest heartache she had ever known.

She was falling in love with a man who wished to have nothing more than a fleeting affair with her. She was losing her heart to a baby she would have to walk away from.

Two tears spilled onto Laura's cheeks as she continued to stare at the pair sleeping so peacefully on the sofa.

John had stated loud and clear that they had absolutely no future together. They were from different worlds, he had declared.

Oh, couldn't he see that wasn't true? Didn't he realize that he was becoming her rainbow wish, the man she wanted to spend the remainder of her days with? Didn't he know that she would love Jeremiah as her own son?

No, John saw none of that lovely picture when he looked at her, because he viewed her through the eyes of a man who believed he was meant to move through life alone.

He was struggling to take on the role of father. He had no desire to add the title of husband to his new challenges.

It would be John and Jeremiah against the world, with no one else allowed to enter their private space.

John would reach a decision as to how to deal with the Wyndhams.

He'd map out a plan whereby he would be able to stay in one place...somewhere...to provide Jeremiah with the stable existence the baby needed.

Piece by piece, John would get his new and turbulent life in order, set things to rights, get on with his future with his son.

And nowhere in that scenario did John Colton envision a place for Laura Bishop. He wouldn't look deep within himself to discover how he might really feel about her, how deep his caring might be, what it might blossom into.

He wouldn't even entertain the concept that he might fall in love with her, have a forever with her as his wife, the mother of his son, because he saw himself as a solitary man.

Think about it, John had said. Think of how much they wanted each other, desired each other, could be together within the walls of that cozy cabin and refuse to address all that awaited them beyond its door.

For a handful of minutes, hours, days—and nights—they could have it all...together.

Laura dashed the tears from her cheeks and wrapped her hands around her elbows as she lifted her chin, her gaze still riveted on the sleeping pair on the sofa.

Could she do it? she wondered, franticness edging into her mind. Could she live out a fantasy, her rainbow wish, for as long as it lasted? Could she bear the pain, the endless tears, when it was all over and she was once again alone?

Think about it.

Laura took a shuddering breath.

Her future stretched before her with a dark cloud hovering over it, so empty, so lonely. She didn't even know where she might find herself, if she'd still be with the Wyndhams or somewhere she couldn't even fathom.

But here, in the now, was John. And Jeremiah.

Think about it? Oh, yes, she most definitely was. She was going to gather her courage and grab hold of the happiness within her reach, rejoice in it, cherish it, for as long as it lasted.

She would be John's lover...his...his wife and Jeremiah's mother until reality shattered the make-believe world within that cabin, broke down the door and entered with its chilling truth.

Jeremiah stirred and whimpered. John didn't open his eyes as he patted the baby's back.

"Daddy's here," John mumbled. "Everything's fine. Daddy's here, Jeremiah."

"And mommy's here, too," Laura whispered amid her tears as Jeremiah settled back to sleep. "Mommy is here, baby."

When Jeremiah woke two hours later, he wiggled, then grabbed John's nose. John jerked awake, then smiled at the baby.

"Hey, sport," he said, "how goes it?"

Laura turned from where she sat on the floor in front of the hearth and smiled.

"You two had a nice nap," she said.

"Yeah," John said, leveling himself to his feet with Jeremiah in his arms. "I think I finally whipped my jet lag. I'm as good as new. This boy needs a dry diaper. We shall return."

"Da, da, da," Jeremiah babbled as the pair left the room.

Laura watched them go, her resolve gaining strength, her decision seeming more right with every beat of her racing heart.

I've thought about it, John, she mentally telegraphed. When he came back into the living room, she would tell him that she would no longer deny her desire for him.

She would agree to his proposal for them to be together, truly together, for as long as it was possible. No strings attached. No commitments. No promises. Just the now.

But what he would *never* know was that she was

falling more in love with him with every passing tick of time.

A knock sounded at the door, startling Laura from her turbulent thoughts. She got to her feet and crossed the room to open the door. Betty stood outside, her arms full of grocery sacks.

"Goodness, let me help you with those," Laura said, reaching for a sack. "Come in out of the cold, Betty. It's getting chillier by the minute out there."

Betty entered the cabin and started toward the kitchen with Laura following.

"We're due for snow," Betty said, placing the sacks on the kitchen table. "I heard it on the radio in the truck when I was driving back from town."

John entered the kitchen, carrying Jeremiah.

"Did I hear the word snow?" John said.

"Yes," Betty said, as she and Laura started emptying the sacks. "We're getting a storm. Do you have enough wood cut and stored in a dry place, John?"

"Yep," he said, nodding. "Wouldn't hurt to bring some more wood inside now, though, if one of you ladies will ride herd on this busy boy."

"Oh, give him to me," Betty said. "I haven't had a chance to get to know this young man."

"Why don't you take Jeremiah in by the fire, Betty," Laura said. "I'll tend to these groceries."

"Fine," Betty said, taking Jeremiah from John. "You should put things away where you want them, anyway, Laura, because this is your kitchen."

Laura's head snapped around and she looked at John at the exact moment he looked at her.

"Yes," Laura said, holding his gaze. "It is my kitchen, isn't it? I should be the one to know where everything is since I'm the cook around here. A woman likes her kitchen just so."

"Yes, indeed," Betty said, then left the kitchen, chattering to Jeremiah as she went.

"Laura?" John said, a questioning expression on his face.

"You'd better put on your jacket before you go out to get more wood," she said. "If you don't, you might catch a cold and give it to Jeremiah. We don't want him to get sick, do we?"

"No," John said, narrowing his eyes. "*We* certainly wouldn't want that to happen, would *we?*" He paused. "Am I supposed to be getting a message here, Laura? Or am I reading too much into this?"

"We'll talk later, John," she said, shifting her gaze to a grocery sack. "We have company at the moment."

"Yeah, *we* do," he said gruffly, then spun around and went to get his jacket.

Time passed quickly as Betty played with Jeremiah while Laura and John watched, the sounds of delighted baby squeals and adult laughter filling the cabin to overflowing.

The wind picked up outside, howling like a hungry beast trying to gain entry.

"Goodness," Betty said finally. "Look at the

time. I'd better be on my way. I certainly did enjoy playing with your son, John. Thank you for sharing him with me.''

"He's something, isn't he?" John said, smiling. "He's a terrific kid, and really smart for someone who hasn't had his first birthday yet. Did you notice how smart he is, Betty?"

Betty laughed as she got to her feet. "Yes, proud daddy, I noticed how smart he is.''

"He learned patty-cake very quickly," Laura said. "We only sang the song to him a few times and he understood what to do.''

"Okay, okay, proud mommy," Betty said, raising both hands. "I hereby declare Jeremiah to be the smartest year-old baby on the face of the earth.''

"Oh, well, I didn't mean to sound like…" Laura started, feeling a warm flush stain her cheeks.

"A proud mommy?" Betty said. "Well, you do. Nothing wrong with that. I'll be the proud auntie, or whatever. Well, I'm off.''

"Betty," Laura said, "I have a big pot of stew on the stove. Why don't you stay and have dinner with us? We'd love to have you join us. Wouldn't we, John?"

"What?" he said. "Oh, sure. You bet.''

"Well, all right," Betty said. "But only if I help get it on the table. I'm not used to being waited on.''

"I hope you're hungry," Laura said as the two women headed for the kitchen. "I made far too much stew. We'll be eating it for days if you don't have a hefty serving.''

We, we, we, John thought, as he watched Laura and Betty leave the living room. Laura must have said *we* a dozen times in the past hours.

Was she letting him know that she'd thought about what he'd said, that she was agreeing to live in the now? Share what they could have together inside that cabin until he could no longer keep the turmoil his life had become beyond the door? Or was that just wishful thinking on his part?

Hell, he didn't know.

John leaned forward from where he sat on the sofa and rolled a ball toward Jeremiah.

Laura *did* sound like a proud mother, he mused, just as much as he sounded like a proud, bragging father. What did *that* mean?

Forget it, he thought dryly. He'd never get the answers to those questions, because he didn't have a clue as to what made women tick, didn't even begin to understand them.

No, if he wanted to know what was going on in Laura's pretty head, he would have to come right out and ask her. And the minute he had her all to himself, he would do exactly that.

Dinner was a noisy, fun-filled event, with Betty relating some tales of John's youthful antics, causing him to groan and Laura to laugh as she hung on every word.

Jeremiah, aware that he had an attentive audience, performed for his admirers, tossing food onto the floor, pushing away the spoon John offered, and sailing the sippy cup across the room.

"Eat," John finally said. *"Now."*

Jeremiah stared at his stern daddy, blinked, then opened his mouth to receive the bite of food on the spoon.

"Well, my goodness," Betty said. "Would you look at that? Nice going, Papa."

"Jeremiah's no dope," Laura said, smiling. "I wouldn't argue with that tone of voice, either."

"Oh, yeah?" John said, cocking an eyebrow at her. "I'll have to remember that."

"Heavens," Betty said, "look out the window. It is really snowing out there. Let's get this kitchen cleaned up, Laura, so I can be on my way while I can still see the path."

"No, no," Laura said, "I'll tend to the kitchen. Would you like John to see you safely home?"

"That isn't necessary," Betty said, getting to her feet. "It's not coming down that hard yet. If I leave now, I'll be fine."

Goodbyes were said, Betty kissed Jeremiah on the top of his head, then she left the cabin. Laura began to clear the table while John fed Jeremiah the last of his dinner.

John glanced out the window, then offered Jeremiah a spoonful of pudding for dessert. The baby swallowed the treat, then leaned forward and opened his mouth.

"Like that, huh?" John said, giving Jeremiah another bite. "Great stuff. Chocolate glue."

The snow was really coming down out there, John thought. Didn't *Laura* realize that she had to go all the way back up to the main house in this weather?

Yeah, well, maybe it just hadn't registered as she concentrated on cleaning the kitchen. The decent, gentlemanly thing to do would be to point out to Laura that she'd best be going while she could be assured of not getting lost in the swirling snow.

The rotten, tricky thing to do would be not to mention the weather until it was too late, then Laura would have no choice but to spend the night in the cabin.

And then?

Well...

"Da, da, da," Jeremiah said, smacking the high chair tray.

"Oops. Sorry." John shoveled more pudding into Jeremiah's mouth.

Da, da, he thought. Daddy. Father. A man whose actions, attitudes, values would be observed by his son as the years went by.

No, Jeremiah wouldn't know if his father purposely kept silent about a snowstorm with the hopes of enticing a special, lovely lady into his bed. But John would know what he had done, and it would be tough to look his little guy in the eye.

Ah, hell.

John wiped Jeremiah's mouth with a napkin, then lifted the baby out of the high chair.

"All finished?" Laura said, glancing over at the pair. She redirected her attention to the sink full of soapy water. "I won't be long here. You could pick a couple of Jeremiah's toys that float and we'll give him a bath after I'm done with the kitchen."

Jeremiah patted John on the cheek and John sighed in defeat.

"Laura," he said, "the snow is covering the path to the house. You should... Well, I mean, don't you think you ought to...leave?"

Laura's hands that were submerged in the water stilled, then she turned her head slowly to look at John.

"Do you want me to?" she said quietly. "Leave? Go back to the house for the night?"

John frowned. "No, you know I don't. I made myself very clear about that, but—"

"You said I should think about it," Laura interrupted, "and I have."

John's heart began to thud rapidly as he looked at Laura intently. Jeremiah wiggled and John set him on the floor, where he began to shred a napkin that had fallen from the table.

"You thought about what I said?" John said. "All of it?"

"About just living in the here and now?" Laura said. "About the fact that we have no chance of a future together, but we do have this little world inside this cabin?" Laura nodded. "Yes, I've thought it all through and I understand the...rules, shall we say."

"And?" John said, hardly breathing.

"It doesn't matter how much it snows, John. I won't be going out in it tonight."

Yes! John's mind hammered. Laura had chosen to stay with him. This was fantastic. They were going to have more than just the one magical night they'd spent together.

Laura was staying.

With *him*.

"You're sure about this?" he said.

"Yes, John, I'm sure." Laura paused. "Jeremiah has a mouth full of paper napkin."

"Oh, geez." John snatched the baby up and began to pull the paper from his mouth. "I can't take my eyes off of you for a second, can I, sport? You are one busy little kid, which is why we parents of superior intelligence own a playpen. Let's go."

Laura watched John leave the kitchen with Jeremiah, then took a shuddering breath.

She'd done it, she thought. She'd committed herself to a no-commitment...affair. Oh, how she hated that tacky word. It wouldn't be an affair. No, to her it would be a fantasy of sorts, the chance to live her rainbow wish for a short time, stolen out of the clutches of reality.

And when it was over?

Stop it, Laura, she told herself as she dunked the big pot into the water. There was nothing to be gained by looking ahead to the bleak and empty future that was waiting for her.

Later that night, when she made love with John, she would exist in the moment at hand...live, and love, and laugh...with John.

Chapter Eight

The following days and nights flew by so quickly that Laura wished she could wave a magic wand and stop time.

It was glorious...all of it.

The snow that had fallen the evening Betty stayed for dinner melted by the next afternoon, except for patches beneath the trees.

Laura put socks on Jeremiah's hands and she and John took the baby outside for his first encounter with the white, cold stuff. Jeremiah was not quite certain he liked the feel of it.

On another day the three drove into town to purchase more diapers, mittens for Jeremiah, a safety seat for the bathtub, and a device for John to strap on his back to hold Jeremiah when they went for walks.

They saw the Reverend Tucker in one of the stores. When the good reverend became as flustered in John's presence as his wife had, John frowned in confusion, then dismissed the episode from his mind when Harold rushed away before John could introduce him to Laura and Jeremiah.

What John did know for sure was that he was becoming more proficient at caring for his son, sensing what needed to be done, then stepping in and doing it.

The days were filled with caring for Jeremiah.

The nights belonged to Laura and John.

On the morning that marked a week since Laura had moved into the cabin, she woke earlier than usual, realizing that it had not been Jeremiah's demanding wail to be rescued from his crib that had brought her from her dreamless sleep.

She turned her head to look at John in the dim light in the bedroom, smiling softly as she gazed at him where he slept on his stomach next to her.

Magnificent, she thought. Even while he slept there was a masculine power emanating from him, a blatant sexuality that caused the embers of desire within her to burn brighter at the mere sight of him.

Oh, how she loved this man.

These days and nights with John had far surpassed the hopes and dreams of her rainbow wish. He was everything and more that she had fantasized about finding in her soul mate.

She sighed and stared up at the ceiling.

They were doing it, just as they'd planned. Not

once during their time together had they spoken of the future, nor had John faced the fact that he was a Wyndham.

They simply existed in the moment, gloried in it, enjoyed Jeremiah, then reached eagerly for each other in the darkness of night.

She had never been so happy, so fulfilled and content.

So foolish.

In quiet solitude such as this, there was nowhere to hide from the truth of what she was doing. When this fantasy ended, she would suffer heartache so intense, it would steal the very breath from her body.

Would the tears she would shed ever end, or would she yearn for John and Jeremiah for the remainder of her days?

Oh, Laura, don't, she admonished herself. The world beyond the cabin door would rush into the magical existence within these walls soon enough, without her dimming the happiness she had by anticipating it.

She sighed again, then pushed the gloomy thoughts away.

"That was a sad sigh," John said, his voice husky with sleep.

Laura jerked at the sudden sound of John's voice and turned her head to smile at him.

"Good morning," she said. "We're both awake before Jeremiah. That's a first."

"Back up to the sad sigh," John said. "What's wrong, Laura?"

''Nothing. I was just...just scolding myself for waking up earlier than I needed to, that's all.''

''Mmm,'' he said, sliding his hand across her stomach. ''I woke up, too, you realize. I think this is one of those unspoken message things.''

''Oh?''

Laura shivered as John moved his hand upward, slowly, tantalizingly, to find one of her breasts. He began to stroke the nipple in a steady, maddening rhythm.

''Yep,'' he said. ''You know, like when you pass me the salt before I ask for it. Or when you turn on the radio to a country-western station just as I was about to get up and do it.''

''Me?'' Laura said, her breath catching as desire thrummed hotter and hotter in her body.

''You know me better than I know myself at times, Laura. You anticipate my wants, my needs... which is why you woke early, then somehow told me that you were awake.''

''Well, I... Well...John, I can't think when you do what you're doing.''

John threw back the blankets and rolled on top of her.

''Don't think,'' he said, close to her lips. ''It's against the law to think this early in the morning. Just feel. Just want...me.''

''Oh, I do,'' she said, sinking her hands into his thick hair. ''I want you, John.'' *I love you, John Colton.*

He captured her mouth in a searing kiss, and passion exploded within them, consuming them instantly.

Laura, John's mind hammered. He would never get enough of her. *Never.* It was as though she'd become a part of him, his other half, her mere presence making him complete, whole.

What did it all mean?

Laura whimpered with need and all rational thought fled from John's mind. He broke the kiss to move lower, drawing one of Laura's breasts into his mouth, laving the nipple with his tongue.

Laura's hands fluttered restlessly over John's broad back, soft fingertips dancing on taut muscles. She savored the sensations surging through her, the heat, the incredible heat, the feel of John's powerful body pressed against her.

Now. Please. John, please, she whispered in her mind. She wanted him. She needed him. Now.

"John," she said, her voice a near-sob.

He raised his head to look directly into her smoky-green eyes, then nodded, his breathing rough.

He left her only long enough to reach in the nightstand drawer for a foil packet, then moments later returned to enter her, filling her, groaning with masculine pleasure as she received all of him.

The rocking rhythm began, slowly at first, then increasing in tempo, harder, faster. Ecstasy. Coils of heat tightened within them as they soared higher, anticipating the moment of exquisite release.

"John!"

"Laura, my Laura."

Rainbows, Laura thought, from a faraway place. There they were, the multitude of beautiful rainbows.

They floated back like feathers caught in a gentle breeze, then settled, holding fast to each other.

"Oh, my," Laura whispered.

John buried his face next to Laura's head on the pillow, catching his weight on his forearms.

"Mmm," he said, his voice muffled. "Oh, yes." He paused. "Let's go back to sleep, then wake up and do this again."

"Mmm," Laura said dreamily.

"Dada. Mama," Jeremiah yelled in the distance, then began to cry.

John chuckled and raised his head. "So much for that great idea."

"Our master's voice," Laura said, smiling. "My sister claims that baby's say dada and mama before they actually know the meaning. Those are just easy sounds for them to make. But if that's true, then why does Jeremiah yell dada and mama when he wants to get up? Oh, well, the day has officially begun."

"To answer your mama-dada question, it's because Jeremiah is a genius. And, no, the day began the moment I opened my eyes and saw you. You're very nice to wake up to, Ms. Bishop."

"So are you, Mr. Colton," she said. So are you, Prince James Wyndham of Wynborough. Darn it, where had that come from? John's true identity and all the complexities it brought were still being kept outside the tightly locked door of the cabin.

Jeremiah's wail increased in volume.

"He's pitching a fit," John said. "I'll get him up while you shower and dress. Then you can finish feeding him his breakfast while I get decent."

"Sounds like a plan," Laura said.

"We're a good team." John brushed his lips over hers. "In fact, there are a few things we are terrific at doing together, ma'am."

John moved off the bed, tugged on a pair of jeans, then headed for the bedroom door.

"I'm hustling, Jeremiah," he called. "Keep your wet diaper on, sport. I'm on my way."

Laura smiled, her heart nearly bursting with love for John and for the baby who was eagerly waiting for his daddy to appear.

After breakfast, Laura cleaned the kitchen, then entered the living room just as John was closing the screen on the fire he had made in the hearth. Jeremiah was standing at the sofa, reaching for a ball on one of the cushions.

"There we go," John said, getting to his feet. "Toasty warm."

At the sound of his father's voice, Jeremiah turned and extended one little hand toward John. In the next moment he lifted the other hand from the sofa and started forward tentatively.

"Oh, my," Laura said. "John, look. Jeremiah is taking his first steps alone."

John spun around, then dropped to one knee, holding out his arms to a teetering Jeremiah.

"That's my boy," John said. "Come on. You can do it, sport."

One step. Two. Three.

Jeremiah lost his balance and began to fall backwards. John leaned forward and scooped him up, rising in the process and hugging the baby.

"Did you see that, Laura?" John said, beaming. "Jeremiah walked. He did it!"

Laura smiled and nodded, unable to speak as tears filled her eyes and closed her throat.

"Man, what a terrific thing to witness," John said, his hold on the baby tightening. "His first steps. I... Whew." He shook his head as his emotions swamped him.

Laura crossed the room and patted Jeremiah gently on the back.

"What a big boy you are," she said, tears still shimmering in her eyes. "I'll never forget this moment. Never."

Jeremiah began to wiggle, protesting the restricting hold his father had on him. John walked to the playpen and placed Jeremiah among the toys. He stared at his son, then turned to meet Laura's gaze.

"It's really hitting me," he said, his voice raspy, "that I might never have known that Jeremiah existed. That's a...a terrifying thought, Laura.

"We just saw him take his first steps. Think of all the firsts he has yet to discover as he grows up. I could have been in a stinking jungle halfway around the globe, not even aware that I had a son."

"Don't dwell on that, John," Laura said, her

voice trembling. "You're here with Jeremiah now, and you'll be with him until he's grown and ready to take on the adventures waiting for him as a man. You're together, just as you should be. You'll see all his…his firsts."

But *she* wouldn't, she thought, struggling against more threatening tears. She would be gone. When reality pounded on the door of the cabin too loudly to be ignored, the magical world she was living in within those walls would be over. Her rainbow wish would be shattered into a million pieces.

John went to the hearth and stared into the leaping flames, his hands shoved into the back pockets of his jeans. A heavy silence fell over the room.

Laura sank onto the sofa, her gaze on John's broad back, wondering what he was thinking. Jeremiah played quietly in the playpen.

Seconds ticked into minutes.

"Do you think," John said finally, his voice low and gritty, "that the Wyndhams saw me take my first steps before…before they believed I…I was dead?"

"Oh, John," Laura said, a sob catching in her throat.

He pulled his hands free of his pockets and turned to look at her, raw pain radiating in the depths of his blue eyes.

"My, God, Laura," he said, "the agony those people went through, the horror. What if Jeremiah was suddenly ripped out of our lives, just disappeared? What if we didn't know where he was, or what was happening to him? Then the word comes that he's dead. He no longer exists. He's gone... forever.''

"No," Laura whispered. Two tears spilled onto her cheeks and she dashed them away with shaking fingertips. "Oh, no, no."

"That's what they suffered through...the Wyndhams," John went on. "Because I have Jeremiah, I'm beginning to understand what they endured."

He stared up at the ceiling for a long moment, willing his raging emotions under control, then he looked at Laura again.

"And now?" he said. "They've discovered that their son *isn't* dead. He's alive, a man grown, a living, breathing entity. *James, their son, is alive.*"

"Yes," Laura said, crying openly, "you *are* alive. They need to see you, touch you, hear your voice, drink in the very essence of you."

"Yes." John shifted his gaze to Jeremiah. "But..." He shook his head.

Laura took a shuddering breath. "But...what?"

John met her gaze again. "I'm their son in the biological sense, Laura, but I'm not Prince James Wyndham of Wynborough. I'm John Colton of...of nowhere. I understand now, I truly do, their need to see me, but I can't be for them what they'll be expecting me to be."

"You can't possibly know what their expectations might be."

"Come on, Laura, get real," he said, his voice rising. "I'm the only son, the heir to the throne or whatever. Hell, do you honestly believe their minds haven't jumped into fast forward, envisioning me as part of the royal family, performing in the role of a damnable prince?''

''I don't know what they're thinking,'' Laura said, flinging out her arms, ''beyond the pure, heartfelt joy of realizing that you're alive.

''Oh, John, can't you just agree to meet the Wyndhams so they can see you with their own eyes?''

''I have to protect my son,'' John yelled. ''Jeremiah is their biological grandson. What if they attempt to stake a legal claim on him? They have the power and the money and... No, he's mine. *Jeremiah doesn't belong to anyone but me.*''

Pain sliced through Laura like the blade of a hot, sharp knife. She wrapped her hands around her elbows and leaned her head on the top of the sofa, closing her eyes.

Jeremiah doesn't belong to anyone but me, her mind echoed. All those things that John had said meant nothing. *We* just saw him take his first steps. What if Jeremiah was suddenly ripped out of *our* lives? What if *we* didn't know where he was?

We. Our.

Jeremiah doesn't belong to anyone but me.

Reality had intruded with all its stark, cold truths, Laura thought miserably. The door to the cabin had been battered down.

She raised her head and looked at John, feeling as though her heart was breaking.

"No one can take your son from you, John," she said quietly. "You and Jeremiah will make a life together wherever you choose it to be. You'll be a family, the two of you, and it will be up to you who will be included in your lives."

She got to her feet, praying her trembling legs would support her.

"You'll realize you have nothing to fear from the Wyndhams once you calm down and think about it," she said. "Now I need to get something out of the freezer to defrost for dinner."

Laura hurried from the room.

John frowned as he watched Laura disappear from his view.

Was Laura upset? he wondered. She seemed tense all of a sudden. Yeah, well, who could blame her? She was probably fed up with his neurotic fears about the Wyndhams possibly staking a claim on Jeremiah, his reluctance to meet his birth parents while at the same time realizing how much they needed to see him, and on the list went.

John slouched onto the sofa, then visually followed the flying path of a red block that came sailing out of the playpen, accompanied by Jeremiah's chortle.

It was all closing in on him, John thought. All that was waiting for him beyond this cabin was demanding its due. This idyllic week with Laura and Jeremiah was coming rapidly to an end.

Damn.

It had been good, more than good. It had been

wonderful. Just Laura and his son, living, laughing, loving. The three of them had been a...a family, during these stolen hours. A family in which he really belonged, was accepted just as he was.

But it was all a fantasy encased in a bubble that was about to burst.

Laura was ready for this cooped-up existence to be over, that was for sure. She'd laid it all out, how he and Jeremiah would be together, just the two of them, wherever he chose to establish a home.

He could have sworn that Laura had been happy during the days...and nights...they'd shared here. So, okay, maybe she *had* been content, but it was because she knew it was temporary. They'd been acting out roles...father, mother, baby. A family.

And he'd liked it.

Hell, he'd more than liked it. It had been as close to perfection as life could get. Waking up each morning next to Laura, tending to Jeremiah with her during the day, making love with her in the darkness of night—fantastic, all of it.

But it was about to be over.

John leaned forward, propped his elbows on his knees and rested steepled fingers against his lips.

Laura was going to walk out of his life, he thought, frowning deeply. The Wyndhams were going to put in an appearance at The Rocking C, no doubt about it. They'd either tell Laura to report back to duty on the island of Wynborough, or release her from her position and send her on her way.

She'd be gone.

He'd never see Laura Bishop again.

He'd never hold her, kiss her, hear her whisper his name in the heat of passion, never again see her smile as she played with Jeremiah.

Damn, he would miss her. The mere thought of her not being by his side was causing a chill to course through him. There would be a void, an emptiness, in his life with nothing—no one—to fill it.

Whoa, Colton, John told himself. Get a grip. He was sounding like some sappy guy who was head over heels in love, for crying out loud. Ridiculous. He wasn't in love with Laura. No way. Sure, he cared for her, very, very much, but love? Not him.

No, he was a loner. Always had been, always would be. He'd shifted emotional gears to make room for Jeremiah in his life, but that was as far as he went.

He'd gotten caught up in the fantasy of this past week, that was all. But it was exactly that...a fantasy. There were no everyday pressures of jobs, and bills, and whose turn it was to give the kid a bath at the end of a long, grueling day.

It had all been a play, and the curtain was coming down on the final act.

Laura would leave, get on with her life. He would make decisions regarding his future plans with Jeremiah. That would be that.

"Mama," Jeremiah called from the playpen. "Mama."

"She's in the kitchen, sport," John said quietly, looking over at the baby.

But she wouldn't be for long. Very soon now they'd have to leave this cabin, close the door on the empty rooms and forget it. Forget everything that had transpired within these walls.

He could—would—do that.

No problem.

Right?

"Right," John said, getting to his feet.

"Rii," Jeremiah said merrily. "Rii, rii."

John chuckled as the baby attempted to repeat what his daddy had said, then spun around as a knock sounded at the cabin door.

Go away, he mentally yelled. Whoever you are, just pack it up and go away. You're not welcome here. Not yet. Damn it, not yet!

The knock was repeated.

Man, he was losing it, he thought, crossing the room. It was probably Betty. Hey, maybe she was delivering some hot-from-the-oven cinnamon rolls.

John opened the door and felt a cold fist tighten in his gut.

"Mitch," he said.

"Hey, little brother," Mitch said, smiling. "Long time, no see. Welcome home." He paused. "May I come in?"

"Oh, yeah, sure." John stepped back so Mitch could enter the cabin, then closed the door. "It's good to see you, Mitch."

The brothers shook hands, then exchanged a quick, male hug that included punches on arms. Mitch shrugged out of his jacket, set it on the back of the sofa, then balanced his Stetson on the top of the coat.

"A hell of a lot has happened since the last time we were together, wouldn't you say?" Mitch said. "It's almost unbelievable."

"No joke," John said, dragging one hand through his hair. "That's the word for it, all right."

"Dada," Jeremiah yelled, pulling himself up to stand in the playpen. "Up."

"Hey, there's my nephew." Mitch crossed the room and lifted Jeremiah into his arms. "Hello there. I understand your name is Jeremiah. I'm your uncle Mitch. And you are a carbon-copy picture of your daddy."

John joined the pair and ruffled Jeremiah's hair.

"He took his first steps alone this morning," John said. "Laura and I saw him do it. It was awesome."

"He's a fine-looking boy, John," Mitch said, "and you're obviously a proud father. Man, I can hardly wait until our baby is born."

"Congratulations on getting married, and expecting a baby and the whole bit," John said. "You, I can picture as a natural father. Me? I'm still winging it with Laura's help."

"Where is Laura?" Mitch said, as Jeremiah tweaked his nose.

"I'm here," Laura said quietly, stepping into the living room. "I'm delighted to see you again, Mitch," she added, producing a small smile.

No, she wasn't, she thought. She wanted him to go back out that door and take reality with him, to allow her to restore the rainbow fantasy within these walls to what it had been. But it was too late for that. Too late.

"How's Alex?" she said. "Even more, where is she?"

"She's up at the house," Mitch said. "She's suffering from morning sickness and is pretty tired from the trip here from Wynborough." He looked at John. "She's very eager to see you, John, but didn't want to appear on your doorstep uninvited.

"She...well, both of us...figure you've had a great deal to adjust to all at once. She'll wait until you're ready to meet her."

"She will?" John said, raising his eyebrows.

Mitch nodded. "Yep. Your sister is a wonderful woman. In fact, all four of your sisters are super people. So are your..." His voice trailed off.

"My parents?" John said, frowning. "The King and Queen of Wynborough? My parents are Cissy and Robert Colton, Mitch." He shook his head. "I'm sorry. That's not fair. I'm still trying to get a handle on all of this."

Mitch laughed. "Me, too. You're about the least princely guy I know. My brother the prince. Whoa."

"Knock it off," John said, laughing in spite of himself. "What do you know? I'm a lousy rancher, but I might be a top-of-the-line prince."

"There you go," Mitch said, smiling. "Hey, Jeremiah, do you have a nose fetish?"

"Yeah, he's into noses," John said. "Sit down, Mitch. Want some coffee?"

"John," Laura said, "I'll take Jeremiah up to the house so you and Mitch can speak privately."

"Hey, no, come on in here," John said. "You and I don't have any secrets between us."

"You and Mitch need some time alone. Besides, Jeremiah's probably ready for a dry diaper. I appreciate your offer to stay, though."

You and I don't have any secrets between us.

But what exactly did they have together? Laura thought as she left the living room with Jeremiah. *Oh, Laura, don't.* She knew the answer to that question. From the moment that Mitch had knocked on the door, all that she and John shared were memories.

Chapter Nine

"So," Mitch said, "what's going on with you and Laura? Betty said that Laura has been living here in the cabin with you and Jeremiah."

"Betty has a big mouth."

"That's not news," Mitch said. "What *is* news is that it would appear that you're smack-dab in the middle of a relationship with Laura Bishop."

John got to his feet, went to the hearth and added an unneeded log to the blazing fire.

"Laura is teaching me how to tend to Jeremiah," he said, closing the screen across the fire.

"Yeah, right," Mitch said. "She could do that by showing up in the morning and heading for the house once Jeremiah is down for the night."

John turned to face his brother.

"This is none of your business, Mitch," he said, frowning.

"Yes, it is. Laura is like a member of the Wyndham family. I'm married to a Wyndham. Hell, John, *you* are a Wyndham. Everything I've heard and know about Laura indicates that she doesn't go in for casual flings. I'd just hate to see her get hurt, that's all."

"Laura and I have an understanding," John said, crossing his arms over his chest. "No one is going to get hurt here, okay? Does that satisfy your need to protect the female populace from men like me?"

"Don't get hostile," Mitch said, raising both hands. "It's just that Laura isn't the type of woman you usually hook up with."

"I'm aware of that, Mitch," John said, narrowing his eyes. "Laura is special, classy, very rare and real, honest and—now you're grinning like a damn fool. What's your problem?"

"Not a thing," Mitch said, still smiling. "Nothing at all."

Laura reentered the room and settled onto the chair by the hearth.

"Jeremiah went down for a nap," she said. "This would be a good time for you to go up to the house to meet Alex, John."

"No," he said quickly. "I mean, Mitch said she's resting."

Mitch got to his feet. "She's not sleeping, though. She just planned to stretch out on the bed for a while. Come on, John, I'm eager for you to meet my lovely wife, and she wants to say hello to her brother-in-law.''

''Damn it, Mitch, I also happen to be her brother, remember?'' John said none too quietly. ''What am I supposed to say to her?''

Mitch shrugged. ''Start with 'It's nice to make your acquaintance.' Just be yourself.''

''Which one? John Colton, or Prince James Wyndham of Wynborough?''

Mitch went to the end of the sofa and picked up his Stetson and jacket.

''That's up to you, isn't it?'' he said. ''No one is going to push you into being something, or someone, you're not, John. We never have, never will. Come on. Let's go.''

John glared at Mitch, the ceiling, Laura, then finally sighed.

''Yeah, all right,'' he said. ''I might as well get this over with. Ten minutes max. Ten minutes, then I'm outta there. Got that?''

''Yep,'' Mitch said, placing his Stetson firmly on his head. ''Ten minutes. Not nine minutes, not eleven…ten. Got it.''

''Good,'' John said gruffly.

Over two hours later, Laura put Jeremiah in his high chair, gave him a cracker, then began to prepare his lunch. What she would normally do by rote required her full concentration, as her mind was centered on what might be taking place up at the house.

Ten minutes max, John had said. That was how

long he'd adamantly stated that he would spend with Alexandra. What on earth could they be discussing for such a long time?

Were they getting along? Was he beginning to embrace his role of Prince James of Wynborough, or was he making it very clear that he wanted no part of his title, or the Wyndham family?

"Oh, Jeremiah, I don't know what's happening up at the house," Laura said, placing pineapple chunks on the high chair tray. "Your father is going to be making decisions that will have a tremendous effect on your future."

Decisions that would have nothing whatsoever to do with *her* future, she thought gloomily. Nothing at all.

Laura settled onto a chair in front of Jeremiah and began to feed him mashed potatoes, tiny pieces of cooked vegetables, and slivers of tender meat. Jeremiah opened his mouth on cue as he smashed the pineapple into a gooey mess on his tray.

The front door opened, then slammed closed, and Laura jumped at the sudden noise. John strode into the kitchen, removing his jacket before tossing it and his Stetson onto a chair at the table.

"I'm sorry, Laura," he said. "The time just got away from me. It wasn't fair to leave you to tend to Jeremiah for this long."

"We're fine, John," she said, looking up at him. "But I couldn't help but wonder how you and Alex were getting along, what you were discussing all this time."

"Do you want me to finish feeding Jeremiah his lunch?" John paused. "What's that gunk on his tray?"

"Pineapple. I'll feed him. Did you like Alex?"

John nodded as he sat down at the table. "Yes, I liked her very much. She's warm, fun, down to earth. She doesn't put on airs about being a princess, and she's obviously very much in love with Mitch. I could tell that they're happy together."

"Open, Jeremiah," Laura said, offering another bite of potato. "And? What did you talk about?" She shook her head. "Well, that's none of my business, I guess. Don't feel you have to tell me."

John frowned. "Why wouldn't I share it with you? We don't have any secrets between us, Laura."

Except the fact that she was in love with him, Laura thought. That was something John Colton would never, ever know.

"Alex said how happy the whole family is to know I'm alive," John said, "then she dropped the subject, didn't dwell on it. She was more interested in my plans for the future."

Laura nodded.

"I guess what it boils down to," John went on, "is that I have two options open to me at the moment. Stay here on The Rocking C, or take Jeremiah to Wynborough."

"Oh."

"I could go anywhere, I guess. It's just that I think Jeremiah deserves to be close to family, not feel...well, isolated while he's growing up. I want him to have a sense of belonging.''

''I see.''

John frowned. ''Could you give me a little more input than 'Oh' and 'I see?'''

Laura gave Jeremiah the last bite of food, then turned to look at John.

''I really don't feel comfortable giving you my opinion, John, because I'm afraid I might influence you in some way. That wouldn't be right, because the decision about where you choose to live and raise Jeremiah has absolutely nothing to do with me.''

Laura got to her feet and hurried to the sink to keep John from seeing the tears that filled her eyes. She turned on the water and washed Jeremiah's bowl and spoon. Then she washed them again, and yet again.

John stared at her, a flood of emotions nearly overwhelming him. He was consumed by a flash of fury at Laura's reluctance to discuss the future, then he was hit by confusion, followed by a chilling pain that tightened like a cold fist in his gut.

Laura was distancing herself from him and from Jeremiah, he thought. She was making it crystal clear that the time the three of them had had together there in the cabin was over.

Mitch had arrived with reality in tow, and Laura was bailing out of the fantasy world within these walls.

It was over. All of it.

He was alone now with his son. It was just the two of them. John and Jeremiah. Or was it James and Jeremiah? Hell, he didn't know. John. James. Colton. Wyndham.

He had so many decisions to make. He valued Laura's opinion, respected her intelligence and levelheaded thinking. Couldn't she help him regarding his choices?

Didn't she care, even a little, where he ended up making a home for Jeremiah?

No, apparently she didn't.

And that hurt. It really hurt.

John got to his feet and extended his arms toward Jeremiah.

"Come on, sport," he said. "I'll wash your face, change your diaper, comb your hair, and take you to meet your aunt Alex. She's a cool lady. You'll like her."

He lifted Jeremiah out of the high chair.

"Dada," the baby said, patting his daddy's nose.

"Please tell Alex that I'll come up to the house later to talk to her," Laura said quietly, still fiddling with the spoon and bowl. "She may know what decision has been reached regarding my position with the Wyndhams.

"I seriously doubt that my services will be needed by the princesses any longer. I'll probably return to Wynborough only long enough to collect my belongings."

"That was subtle," John said heatedly. "In other words, you're letting me know that if I decide to make a home for Jeremiah on Wynborough, you won't be there.''

"I—"

"No, let's make it clearer than that, shall we?" John said. "Even if you continue to be employed by the Wyndhams and you stay on the island, you wouldn't be there for *me*.''

Laura shut off the water and turned to look at John.

"Be there for you for what purpose, John?'' she said, her voice trembling slightly. "To continue our affair? To engage in good, old-fashioned lusty sex on demand, with no commitments, no promises?

"I agreed to that only for the duration of our stay in this cabin, John, but it's over. It's time to move forward, each going our separate way.''

John set Jeremiah on the floor, then strode across the room to grip Laura's upper arms.

"Lusty sex?" he said, a muscle jumping in his jaw. "Has what we've shared been that for you? Sex? I thought we were making love, Laura. My mistake, huh? It was just wham, bam, thank-you, ma'am, right? Stud service.''

"Oh, John, don't,'' Laura said, shaking her head. "Please. What we've shared here in this cabin has been so special and beautiful. But we both knew from the outset that it was all time stolen out of reality.''

She took a shuddering breath.

"You said yourself,'' she went on, "that we don't have any chance of a future together because we come from different worlds. Being with you this past week has emphasized that truth.''

''I...'' John started.

''Please, let me finish,'' Laura said, looking directly into his eyes. ''I have my rainbow wish tucked away in the part of my heart that holds hopes and dreams. I want it all...a husband, children, a home filled with love and laughter.

''I may never achieve that dream, but I won't compromise myself by settling for less and somehow making it all right. I won't have an ongoing affair with a man who moves through life alone, one who has managed to include his son in that life, but who doesn't want, need, nor have room for anyone else.''

''But, Laura—''

''No,'' she said, tears filling her eyes. ''Don't say anything, because there's nothing more to be said. Yes, we made love here in our fantasy world, and I plan to cherish those memories. You can keep them, or erase them from your mind. That's up to you.

''But, John, when Mitch knocked on the door of this cabin, then came inside, he brought reality with him. What we had, shared, is over. I'm...I'm moving back up to the house today to learn where my career stands with the Wyndhams.''

''You're leaving the cabin?'' John said, his hold on her tightening. ''What about Jeremiah?''

''You're perfectly capable of caring for him on your own now,'' Laura said, blinking away her tears. "You know you are. You don't need me here any longer. You don't need me, John."

Laura pulled free of John's hands and hurried out of the kitchen. John turned to watch her go, his heart thundering painfully.

"Mama," Jeremiah whined, extending his arms in the direction that Laura had gone. "Dada. Doggy."

John crossed the room and lifted Jeremiah from the floor.

"Daddy's here, Jeremiah," he said, patting the baby on the back. "It's just the two of us, sport, you and me. We'll be fine, you'll see. Just fine."

You don't need me, John.

Laura's words echoed in his mind and he frowned.

Was that true? Yes, he supposed it was. To really *need* someone was part of being in love. He would never fall in love because he didn't know how to open his heart.

Yes, he loved Jeremiah, but that came from a different place, required nothing more of him than to just be. Jeremiah's trust in him was innocent and unconditional. John couldn't fall short because his son had no preconceived ideas of what a father should do.

But a woman? Laura?

She'd given him so much. With her he'd felt complete, had savored the sense of rightness, of belonging, in their fantasy world.

But he'd given her nothing in return.

He wasn't the man to fulfill Laura's rainbow wish. He could never come to love her the way she deserved to be loved because he wasn't capable of doing that.

He just didn't know how.

Chapter Ten

Late that night Laura lay in bed unable to sleep. She was once again in the room she had chosen to use in the main house on The Rocking C.

Same ranch, she thought. Same house. Same bed. But, oh, merciful saints, she was not remotely close to being the same Laura Bishop who had agreed to wait for the return of John Colton to the family home.

She was now a woman who was in love with a man who didn't love her in return.

Oh, how difficult it had been to collect her belongings and walk out of that little cabin in the woods. She had left behind the man and the baby who had stolen her heart for all time.

She was so alone and lonely, had wept in the

privacy of her room until her head throbbed, her eyes were puffy and red, and she had no tears left to shed.

But her heartache was her own fault. She knew it and was furious at herself for her lack of emotional sophistication. She hadn't been strong enough, worldly enough, to engage in an affair, then go blissfully on her way when it was over.

No, not her. She'd fallen in love with the man she'd agreed to have a brief fling with, missed him so much that her heart actually physically hurt.

She was such a ninny. A starry-eyed, romantic child masquerading in a woman's body. She'd know from the beginning that John Colton was a solitary man, a loner, who wanted nothing to do with the convention of hearth and home, wife and babies.

Granted, he'd shifted emotional gears very quickly to include Jeremiah in his life, to truly love his son. But John had stopped there and would go no further. There was no place in his life for a wife, or a mother for Jeremiah.

"I knew that," Laura said aloud.

It wasn't John's fault that her heart was smashed to smithereens. She had no one but herself to blame for her misery.

Laura sighed.

The hours of the evening had seemed endless, as though she was never going to be able to escape to the sanctuary of her room.

Yes, it had been nice to see Alexandra again and

to hear all the glorious details of Elizabeth and Rafe's beautiful wedding.

Yes, it was reassuring to hear Alex say that Laura's services with the Wyndhams were still very much needed. Alex's parents would require more assistance than they presently had as they continued to prepare for King Phillip's coronation celebration and took on the social functions previously performed by their married daughters.

Yes, it had been wonderful to witness again the genuine love between Alex and Mitch, to see Alex literally glowing as a wife and mother-to-be.

Except...

Watching Alex and Mitch together had emphasized Laura's chilling loneliness. She had wanted to dash through the woods, enter the cabin, fling herself into John's arms and tell him she'd stay by his side forever under any circumstances.

"No, no, no," Laura whispered, pressing her fingertips to her throbbing temples.

She could not—would not—settle for less than her rainbow wish.

And that wish was not going to be fulfilled by John Colton, Prince James Wyndham of Wynborough.

James Wyndham. Dear heaven, what if John decided to raise Jeremiah on the island of Wynborough? How could she bear to be so close to John and Jeremiah, yet be so removed from their lives?

No. She had enough grief to deal with without letting her imagination heap more on her plate. She wouldn't dwell on the possibility of John moving to Wynborough. She'd wait until he made a decision regarding his and Jeremiah's future, then make her own choices as to what to do.

Somehow...somehow, Laura thought sleepily, she had to figure out what was the best thing for *her* to do.

At last exhaustion claimed her, and she drifted off into a restless slumber.

John smoothed the blanket over Jeremiah, then stood quietly by the crib, losing track of time as he watched his son sleep.

With a sigh, John finally turned, left the room and wandered into the living room. He slouched onto the sofa, stretched his jeans-clad legs out in front of him and stared into the glowing embers of the ebbing fire in the hearth.

He couldn't sleep, had tossed and turned until the sheets on the bed were a tangled mess. After yanking on his jeans, he'd gone to check on Jeremiah, but now couldn't face returning to that empty bed.

"Damn," he said.

He missed Laura. There it was. Bottom line. Pure and simple.

The entire evening had been difficult to get through without Laura there sharing it all with him and Jeremiah. He'd made a decent dinner from leftovers he found in the refrigerator, played with Jeremiah, bathed him, read him a story and put him to bed, acutely aware every moment that Laura wasn't there.

Once Jeremiah had been asleep, the loneliness had hit him like a ton of bricks. The walls of the cabin had seemed to close in on him, crushing him, taunting him with the knowledge that he was alone.

John dragged both hands down his face.

This was crazy. He'd spent his entire adult life alone, had preferred it that way, had functioned just fine on his own with no one demanding his time and attention.

He completed each top-secret assignment he was directed to take on, then waited for new orders to reach him.

But then, everything changed.

His world, his life as he knew it, had been turned inside out when he'd received word of Jeremiah's existence. He'd sent a telegram to the powers-that-be, stating that he was resigning immediately, and then he'd come home to claim his son.

And on the night before he saw and held Jeremiah for the first time, he'd met Laura Bishop in Jake's Saloon.

Lovely Laura. So honest and real, she was able to touch him deep within like no woman before. How right it had all been; the sharing of his inner-most thoughts and fears, the pouring out of his most private feelings.

And how very, *very* right it had been to make love with Laura that night. So rare and beautiful, it had been. All of it.

The fantasy should have ended with the light of dawn. He should have been able to walk away, knowing he'd never see Laura again, savoring the memories of an incredible night with a fantastic and unique woman.

He would have been John Colton of the Rocking C Coltons. A man who was now a single father and who was determined to do the very best job he could in that daunting new role.

He would have focused his entire attention and emotional energies on being a daddy, determining where to raise Jeremiah, how to make a living as he established roots for himself and his son.

That whole scenario would have been a tremendous challenge, an all-consuming endeavor.

''Hell,'' John muttered, ''that was just the tip of the iceberg.''

Now? What a mess. Laura had still been very much in his life in the light of the new day. He'd been slam-dunked by the disclosure that he wasn't just John Colton of The Rocking C Ranch, but Prince James Wyndham of Wynborough. He had another set of parents, four sisters, brothers-in-law, a fancy title and...

And raging emotions centered on Laura Bishop that left him drained and confused beyond measure.

Too much was happening to him too quickly, John thought, shaking his head. He was running in mental circles, accomplishing nothing more than exhausting his brain.

One minute, he wanted to snatch Jeremiah up and

head out, just disappear to somewhere they couldn't be found.

In the next breath, he was chatting comfortably with Alexandra, his *sister,* about the possibility of taking Jeremiah to Wynborough. During that conversation he had been—had felt like—James Wyndham.

John Colton. James Wyndham. The Rocking C. The island of Wynborough. Back and forth, like a never-ending, maddening Ping-Pong game that was driving him right out of his mind.

And through it all, from before Mitch had knocked on the cabin door with reality in tow and after, Laura had been there by his side, sharing it all.

Together, they'd seen Jeremiah take his first steps.

Together, they'd responded as Jeremiah lifted his little arms and called for Dada, or Mama, or Doggy, or his ball.

Together, they'd made exquisitely beautiful love when the time came for them to be woman and man, instead of mother and father.

"Mother," John said aloud. "Jeremiah's mother."

Laura was a wonderful, natural, loving mother to his son. The week the three of them had spent in that cabin had been perfection. John, the father. Laura, the mother. Jeremiah, the baby. Just like the three bears in the fairy tale.

But there was the kicker. It was all a fantasy.

And now it was over.

For Laura to truly have the title of Jeremiah's mother, she should be his wife. They should be married, exchange vows to love each other until death parted them.

But that would never happen because he didn't know how to love like that, didn't know how to be a husband, how to make someone happy.

Even if he was in love with Laura right now, and he didn't have a clue as to whether or not that was true, he wouldn't dare do one thing about it. He couldn't begin to be for Laura what she deserved.

No matter what the Coltons had told him all these years, he knew—damn it, he knew—that he'd fallen short as a son and brother. If he acknowledged his identity as James Wyndham, he'd fail that family, too, just wouldn't measure up to being what they wanted, needed, him to be.

He just didn't know how to love deeply enough to really connect, to give as much as he took.

That cold, glaring flaw that was part of who he was meant that he had no future with Laura, no matter what his true feelings for her might be. She was out of his reach forever.

He was who he was...and it wasn't enough.

John leaned forward and picked up a red ball that was visible on the floor in the soft glow of the embers of the fire. He turned the ball around and around in his hands, staring at it, as new and strange thoughts began to sift slowly into his mind.

A child's toy. He'd never held a child's toy before, but now this small red ball was a familiar object.

He knew how fast to roll it to Jeremiah and how the baby would react when the ball reached him.

He knew the ball was a safe toy, made of material that Jeremiah could chomp on without pieces of it becoming loose to possibly choke him.

He knew that to play with that ball with Jeremiah made his son happy, caused the little boy to laugh in delight and clap his tiny hands.

He knew all those important facts about a small red ball because inch by inch, day by day, he was *learning* how to be a loving father.

John stiffened, dropped the ball and heard the echo of his suddenly thundering heart in his ears. A trickle of sweat ran down his bare chest.

Was it possible that a man like him could *learn* how to truly love a woman like Laura? Could he *learn* to be all that she deserved to have in her partner in life? Could he make her happy? *Learn* how to give as much as he took?

Was there a chance that he wouldn't live out his life alone, without Laura by his side?

''Whoa. Wait,'' John said, shaking his head. ''Whoa, Colton.''

First things first. Before he went any further with this crazy business, he'd better figure out just how deeply his feelings for Laura went.

How did a man know if he was in love?

He didn't have a clue as to the answer to that one. But he knew someone who did...Mitch.

John got to his feet and headed back to bed.

He was definitely certifiably insane. Heaven knew, he had enough on his plate to deal with and here he was serving himself up a heap of emotional questions he was now determined to find the answers to. Nuts. He was totally nuts.

In the bedroom John stripped off his jeans, pulled the sheets into a semblance of order and stretched out on the bed.

As he drew the blanket over him, exhaustion began to creep over his senses.

If someone had told him a few weeks ago that he would be a father who loved his baby son beyond description, he would have laughed himself silly.

But here he was, he thought foggily. He was Jeremiah's daddy and savoring, cherishing, every minute of his new role. Not only that, he wasn't doing a halfway bad job as a father because he was *learning* how to sense, then meet, his son's needs.

Maybe, just maybe, he was capable of more. Maybe, just maybe, if he was actually in love with Laura Bishop, he could continue to grow and change.

Maybe it wasn't too late for him to learn how to love.

John slept, and dreamed of Laura.

The next day was surprisingly warm with a brilliant blue sky and a golden globe of a sun.

In the early afternoon, John stood by one of the white-fenced corrals and watched Mitch walking a horse inside the enclosure with Jeremiah perched in front of him on the saddle.

"Not so fast," John said.

"If I go any slower," Mitch said, "this animal will fall asleep. I'm holding on to Jeremiah, John. We're doing fine here. Say 'horse,' Jeremiah."

"Horse," Jeremiah yelled. "Horse. Horse."

John chuckled. "Yep, that's a horse, in all its ugly glory."

"You should be doing this with your boy, John," Mitch said.

"Forget it," John said. "I never liked those beasts and they never liked me."

"Well, don't blame me if I turn your kid into a rancher, little brother. Jeremiah is really having a grand old time up here."

"Jeremiah will be free to be whatever he wants, whatever he needs, to be happy," John said quietly.

"That's the Colton philosophy," Mitch said. "You're proof of that."

"Yeah, I know," John said. "I'm starting to get the picture of how much you and our parents...well, love me, and showed that love by letting me go when I needed to leave."

Mitch drew the horse to a stop by John and handed Jeremiah over the fence.

"Horse," Jeremiah hollered.

"That's enough for one day," John said, setting Jeremiah on his feet.

Jeremiah grabbed the corral slat, then dropped to his bottom and began to pull handfuls of scrub grass out of the ground. Mitch swung down from the saddle.

"He's a great kid, John," Mitch said.

"Yeah, he is." John paused. "Mitch, I want to ask you something. This is just between us. Okay?"

Mitch folded his arms on the top rung of the fence. "Sure."

"I was just wondering… What I mean is…" John frowned and cleared his throat. "All right, here it is. How did you know, *really know,* that you were in love with Alex?"

Mitch looked at John for a long moment, then nodded.

"Well, I'll tell you, John, in some ways it's so complicated, it boggles the mind. But in other ways it's beautifully simple."

"Cut to the chase," John said gruffly.

"Right. You miss her when you're not with her," Mitch said, "and anticipate the very second that you'll see her again. You feel…complete somehow, whole, not having realized until she came into your life that something was missing."

"Oh…man," John said, staring at his brother.

"Lovemaking is far beyond anything you've previously experienced," Mitch went on. "You automatically think in terms of 'we,' of what you'll do 'together' today, tomorrow, forever. You know you would put your life on the line for her, die if need be, to keep her out of harm's way."

John nodded, hardly breathing.

"And, John?" Mitch said. "When her face lights

up with a smile because you did nothing more than walk into the room, you feel ten feet tall. *You* made her happy just by...by being there. That, brother, is love in its purest, wondrous form.''

''Oh...hell,'' John said, letting out a pent-up breath.

''You're in love with Laura Bishop.''

''I didn't say that,'' John said, glaring at him.

''You didn't have to,'' Mitch said, smiling. ''So? What are you going to do about it?''

John looked down at Jeremiah to be certain that the baby wasn't eating the grass he was still busily yanking up, then met Mitch's gaze again.

''Don't get carried away, Mitch. Alex obviously felt all those things about you. And another thing... how do you plan to *keep* making her happy, *keep* it all so special? How does a man remain in love until he dies?''

''One day at a time,'' Mitch said. ''Just the way our parents are doing it.'' He paused. ''In your case, both sets of your parents. Gabriella and Phillip are very much in love. You can see it, sense it, when you're with them.''

''I've got a knot in my gut that says I'm treading on turf where I don't belong,'' John said.

''It's terrifying at times, no doubt about it,'' Mitch said, nodding. ''But worth it? You'd better believe it. Don't let the fears keep you from going after what you want, John.''

''Yeah, well, like I said, Alexandra loves you in return.''

"How do you know that Laura isn't in love with you?" Mitch said, raising his eyebrows.

"She as much as said so," he said. "You know, saying that what we'd shared was over, it was time to go our separate ways, the whole nine yards."

"All of that sounds more like what *you* might say," Mitch said. "Are you certain she wasn't just echoing what she believes *you* feel?"

John opened his mouth to reply, snapped it closed again and frowned.

"Only one way to find out," Mitch said. "It's time you went courting, little brother."

"Think so?"

"Know so."

"Mitch, I'm not like you, or our folks. Do you really believe that a solitary man like me could learn how to love, do it right?"

"Dada," Jeremiah said, raising his arms.

John bent down and scooped up the baby.

"There's the answer to that question," Mitch said, tipping his head toward Jeremiah.

John shook his head and sighed. "My mind's on red-alert overload."

"I don't doubt that, considering everything you're dealing with all of a sudden," Mitch said. "But I've got twenty bucks that says your heart is on overload, too. And that, brother mine, is the best thing that has ever happened to you."

Chapter Eleven

John returned to the cabin and settled Jeremiah in the crib for his afternoon nap. When the baby had been asleep for about an hour, a knock sounded at the cabin door. John crossed the room to answer the summons.

"Laura," he said, unable to curb the delighted smile that broke across his face.

"Hello, John," she said quietly.

"Come in, come in," he said, stepping back to allow her to enter.

Laura hesitated a moment, then stepped into the living room. John stared at her intently.

Was he in love with this woman? he wondered frantically. Everything that Mitch had clicked off had sure as hell rung true in regard to how he felt about Laura.

And how did Laura truly feel about him? She wanted, needed, her rainbow wish, that much he knew. But was that wish of a loving husband, a soul mate forever, a home and babies, centered on him despite what she'd said about everything they'd shared being over?

Had Laura been echoing the ground rules he'd laid out regarding their relationship as Mitch had suggested might be the case?

How was he going to find the answer about how deeply Laura cared for him? He couldn't just open his mouth and say, ''Hey, Laura, do you happen to be in love with me? The evidence is stacking up pretty high as far as me probably being in love with you, so I'd really like to know if—'' Cripe. That was nuts. This was going to call for some finesse, some fancy footwork.

''Would you like to sit down?'' John said, sweeping one arm through the air.

''No, thank you. I just came to deliver a message,'' Laura said, not looking at him. ''Betty asked me to come because she's busy with preparations for dinner.''

''Oh. What's the message?''

''Elizabeth and Rafe just arrived at the house.''

''Who?'' John said, frowning.

''Your...your sister, Elizabeth, and her husband, Rafe Thorton. They were just married. Remember?''

''Oh, yeah, sure,'' he said, nodding. ''Everyone went to Wynborough for the wedding while you stayed on The Rocking C to wait for me.'' He paused. "Why aren't Elizabeth and Rafe on their honeymoon somewhere?"

"Rafe owns a construction company here in Arizona. They came to The Rocking C to meet you," Laura said, still not meeting John's gaze.

"Oh. Well, all right, but I can't leave the cabin now. Jeremiah is napping."

"Betty would like you and Jeremiah to join everyone for dinner at the house. You could come as soon as Jeremiah wakes up."

"Okay," John said.

"Good. 'Bye." Laura spun around and started toward the door.

"Laura, wait," John said.

She turned to look at him. "Yes?"

"Couldn't you sit down and talk for a minute?"

"About what?" she said, frowning.

"About...um...yes, Jeremiah's birthday." John smiled. "He'll be a year old next week. We ought to plan a party for him, don't you think? You know, cake, ice cream, balloons...yeah, balloons are important...and presents, lots of loot. We need to get organized. It's not every day of the week that a kid turns one. We have to decide—"

"John, don't," Laura interrupted. "Please...just don't."

"Don't what?" he said, obviously confused.

"Don't keep saying 'we,'" she said, her voice trembling slightly. "You and I are not a 'we.' If you want to have a birthday party for Jeremiah, fine, but..." She shook her head as tears began to pool in her eyes.

Oh, no, John thought, look what he'd done. Laura was about to cry. He'd caused her to be that unhappy? She was upset because he'd used the word 'we?' Did this make sense?

He'd been talking about Jeremiah's birthday party, for Pete's sake. He was obviously missing something here. He just didn't get it, didn't understand.

Boy, he sure had illusions of grandeur. He was learning how to be a father so he'd believed he could learn how to love a woman like Laura, make her happy, make her smile.

But the first time he opened his big mouth, he'd caused Laura to be a breath away from bursting into tears.

John dragged one hand through his hair and frowned.

"I'm sorry, Laura," he said quietly. "I wouldn't intentionally upset you, not for the world, but I obviously have. I don't know why you're so unhappy all of a sudden, but I'm the cause of it and I apologize.

"I just thought you might like to be part of putting together Jeremiah's first birthday party, that's all. But, hey, that's okay. I'll ask Betty to bake a cake, and...I'll handle the details and... You'll come, though, won't you? Be there to see Jeremiah open his presents, the whole bit? I would...well, I'd really like you to be there."

Oh, dear, Laura thought, she loved this man so much. She'd overreacted to the simple little word 'we,' and John was scrambling to make amends while not having a clue as to why she was falling apart.

He was so confused, so sweet, so endearing. All he was trying to do was make plans to celebrate his son's first birthday.

"Oh, John, I'm the one who is sorry," Laura said. "You didn't do anything wrong, you truly didn't. I'd be honored to help you with Jeremiah's party."

John smiled. "You would? Are you sure?"

"Yes," she said, matching his smile.

John closed the distance between them and framed Laura's face in his hands.

"Laura, tell me why you were about to cry when I brought up the subject of the party. Please? Talk to me. I'm attempting to understand what happened here. This is us, remember? We share. No secrets."

Laura took a wobbly breath. "Well, the heck with my pride, I guess. I miss you and Jeremiah, John. I miss the fantasy world we had together in this cabin. I knew all along that it would end, but it has been difficult nonetheless."

"I miss you, too," he said, gazing directly into her eyes. "Jeremiah has been looking for you, calling for mama. Ah, hell, Laura, what we shared here doesn't have to be over."

"Yes, it does." Laura stepped back, forcing John to drop his hands from her face. "I'll be leaving in a few weeks to be in Wynborough for the anniversary celebration of King Phillip's coronation.

"Are you getting this, John? I'm leaving. Even if you decide to acknowledge that you're Prince James Wyndham and choose to raise Jeremiah in Wynborough, there is no magical cabin for us on that island. Reality check, John. What we had together within these walls is over."

"Not yet," he said, his voice rising. He needed time to determine if Laura loved him and if he truly loved her. He needed time to find out if there was a glimmer of hope that he could learn how to love, how to make Laura happy. "It's not over yet."

"Yes, it is," she said, nearly yelling. "I won't step back into that fantasy world, because it's too hard to walk away from it. I've cried my tears. I'm looking to the future now, just as you are. You'll be with Jeremiah and I'll...I'll be...alone."

She shook her head.

"There's no point in discussing this further," she said. "Come to the house to meet Elizabeth and Rafe when Jeremiah wakes up."

Laura went to the door, but before she could leave the cabin, John strode forward and flattened one hand on the door, making it impossible for Laura to open it.

She spun around, anger flashing in her green eyes. John smacked his other hand onto the door, trapping her between his arms and moving to within inches of her.

"Did it ever occur to you," he said, his voice

very low and very male, "that what we feel for each other isn't a fantasy? That it's the real goods? What if that's true, Laura? What then?"

Her love for John Colton *wasn't* a fantasy, Laura thought frantically. It was real, and rich, and forever. What was John saying? That he might care for her more than he'd thought? Fine. Dandy. *But it wasn't enough.* She wanted, needed, it all. Her rainbow wish.

"Laura?"

"You said it yourself, John," she said softly. "We're traveling on different roads through life."

"Your road leads to your rainbow."

"Yes. I won't settle for less."

John nodded. "Nor should you. Laura, do you...are you...Laura, do you love me? Are you in love with me?"

Laura narrowed her eyes, placed both hands on John's chest and shoved with all her strength. He staggered backward, his eyes widened in shock.

"Oh, you are despicable, John Colton," she said. "Why do you want to know if I'm in love with you? Is it scorecard time? Are you hoping to put another notch on your make 'em love me, then leave 'em belt?"

"Just answer the damn question," John yelled.

"You want an answer? Well, how's this? Whatever I felt for you, I'll get over it. You bet your sweet bippy I will."

She lifted her chin.

"In fact, I've already started to do that," she said,

none too quietly. "Yes, I certainly have. Love not nurtured just disappears—poof, it's gone. Over and out. Finished. Done."

She pointed one finger in the air.

"I'll be like someone who has had a flu shot. I'll be totally immune to you, John. Yes, that's how it will be. I'll help you with Jeremiah's birthday party, eat dinner at the same table with you up at the house...I'll even live in Wynborough, with you somewhere on the island if you choose to go there."

Laura nodded decisively.

"Hey, no problem, because I'm on the way to recovering from losing my heart to you. In short, Mr. Colton, I'm taking my heart *back,* and nothing you do, or say, will ever be able to touch it again. Any questions?"

John pursed his lips, ran his hand over the back of his neck, then finally said, "Just one."

"What is it?"

"Do you really think," he said, grinning, "that I have a sweet bippy?"

"Aaak!" Laura screamed. "You're insane, John Colton, James Wyndham—whoever you are!"

Laura yanked open the door, then slammed it behind her. Jeremiah's loud wail sliced through the air.

Dinner at the house was a fun, boisterous affair, with two or three conversations continually taking place at the same time.

Laura waited to see where John placed Jeremiah's high chair, then slid onto a chair at the opposite end

of the table. She forced herself to pay attention and
join in the chatter, while struggling to eat the delicious food Betty had prepared.

What she did *not* do was look at John Colton.

She was so mortified, she thought miserably, she
could die. John had pushed, and due to her vulnerable emotional state, she'd blurted out that she'd lost
her heart to him. She was so angry with herself, she
could spit.

Maybe she should leave The Rocking C now, return to Wynborough ahead of the schedule that Elizabeth had presented to her. But if she did, she'd miss
Jeremiah's birthday party and she really wanted to
be there to watch the baby celebrate turning one year
old.

Oh, how was she going to survive being in close
proximity to John while planning the party now that
he knew the depths of her feelings? It would be so
embarrassing, so...

No, now wait a minute. She'd stated...well,
yelled actually...that she was already in the process
of getting over John, dismissing her feelings for him
and moving forward.

What a crock. But John didn't know that. She'd
fake it, bluff her way through the whole thing and
glue her demolished pride back together. Yes, that
was the ticket.

"Right, Laura?" John said from the far end of
the long table.

"What?" she said. "Pardon me?"

"We're going to put on a great party for Jeremiah's birthday,'' John said. ''We're going to have cake, presents, balloons, the whole enchilada.''

''Oh,'' she said, not looking directly at him. ''Yes, we are. It'll be fun.''

Alexandra laughed. ''You sound like you're planning a trip to the dentist, not a birthday party, Laura.''

''I have a headache,'' Laura said, tapping her nose with one finger. ''Sinus trouble.'' She paused. ''In fact, if you'll all excuse me, I believe I'll take my throbbing little head to bed.'' She got to her feet. ''Good night.''

''Mama,'' Jeremiah said, raising his arms. ''Mama.'' He started to cry. ''Ma-a-a-ma.''

Everyone at the table looked at Laura, then looked at each other.

''Your daddy will hold you, Jeremiah,'' Laura said. ''He's tired of being in the high chair, John.'' She glanced around the table. ''Jeremiah isn't really calling me Mama, as in my being his mother. Sometimes I'm Doggy or book or...'' She looked at John. ''Your son wants out of that high chair, John.''

John leaned back in his chair and folded his arms across his chest.

''I'm not the one he wants at the moment, Laura,'' he said. ''You'd better come get him before he hollers the roof down and spoils this festive meal.''

Laura shot John a dark glare, then stomped around the table and lifted Jeremiah into her arms.

The baby stopped crying instantly and laid his head on Laura's shoulder.

She held him tightly, inhaling his sweet aroma, savoring the feel of his solid little body pressed against her. In the next moment she frowned.

"He's awfully warm." She shifted Jeremiah in her arms so she could place one hand on his forehead. "I think he has a temperature. Look how flushed his cheeks are."

John jumped to his feet, nearly knocking over his chair in the process.

"He's sick?" he said. "How sick? What's wrong with him? I'll call the doctor. What doctor? Mitch, who's the doctor in Hope?"

"John, for heaven's sake, calm down," Laura said. "Jeremiah probably has a little cold, that's all. Take him to the cabin, give him a tepid bath and the dosage of baby aspirin that's on the bottle. Keep him warm and make sure he has plenty to drink. He'll be fine."

"Oh," John said. "Yeah, all right."

He placed his hands on Jeremiah's waist to take him from Laura, but the baby wrapped his arms around Laura's neck and began to cry again.

"Jeremiah has spoken," Mitch said, smiling. "You've got a smart kid there, John. He wants a woman's tender touch when he doesn't feel good. Mama Laura, I think you're on duty. Unless, of course, your head hurts too badly to tend to that poor, sick little kid."

Alex poked Mitch in the ribs as she smothered her laughter with a napkin.

"Of course I'll take care of him," Laura said, tightening her hold on Jeremiah.

"Thought you might," Mitch said under his breath.

"John, get our coats," Laura said. "Hush now, Jeremiah. Everything is all right, sweetheart."

As Laura, Jeremiah and John left the room, the quartet at the table exchanged satisfied and knowing smiles.

John finished straightening the bathroom from the bath that Laura had given Jeremiah, then walked into the living room. He stopped, his heart thundering as he drank in the sight before him.

The only luminescence in the room came from the leaping flames of the fire in the hearth.

Laura sat in the chair close to the fireplace, humming softly as she gave Jeremiah a bottle of juice. The baby was snuggled in her arms, wearing a sleeper and wrapped in a fluffy blanket. The glow of the fire poured over the pair like a golden waterfall created just for them.

And at that moment, as John stared at the woman and child, mother and baby, he knew he was deeply and irrevocably in love with Laura Bishop.

He waited for the fear to assault him, the sense of being smothered, the feeling of inadequacy at even presuming that he might be able to make Laura happy, be able to love her as she deserved to be loved, be able to give as much as he took.

Be able to make her rainbow wish come true.

But all he felt was the greatest joy, and the greatest inner peace, and the greatest sense of belonging he had ever known.

Laura glanced over at him. "What's wrong?"

He crossed the room and hunkered down by the chair where Laura sat holding Jeremiah.

"Nothing," he said quietly, looking directly into Laura's eyes. "Nothing is wrong. In fact, things are probably more *right* than they've ever been in my entire life."

"Oh?"

Tell her, Colton, John told himself. *Tell Laura that you love her. Tell her.*

Jeremiah squirmed, jerked his head away from the bottle and began to whine.

"How is he?" John said.

"He's not all that sick, John," Laura said. "His temperature is just under a hundred. He just feels crummy enough to be fussy."

"Crabby, huh?"

"Yes. Here, Jeremiah, have some more juice. You just want to be held and pampered, don't you, sweetheart? Well, that's fine. We all have days like that."

John placed his hands on his thighs and pushed himself to his feet.

This wasn't the time to have a serious discussion with Laura, he decided. She was focused on Jeremiah, which was how it should be while the baby wasn't up to par. So, he'd wait.

John sank onto the sofa and stared at Laura.

Son-of-a-gun, he thought, his heart kicking up a notch again. He was going to do it. He really was. He was going to ask Laura to marry him, to be his partner for life and also to be Jeremiah's mother.

"You're not upset about Jeremiah, are you?" Laura said as she looked at him curiously.

"No, no. If you say he's not very sick, then that's that. I trust you, Laura." John paused. "But then I guess I trusted you from the moment we met in Jake's Saloon, didn't I?"

"That seems like a long time ago," Laura said softly, meeting John's gaze in the glow of the firelight.

"Yeah, a great deal has happened since that night," he said, "but it doesn't diminish how special it was. The days, nights, here in the cabin…you, me, Jeremiah."

"Yes, but—"

"Don't." John leaned forward and propped his elbows on his knees, entwining his fingers. "Don't say, 'Yes, but it's over.' Just don't say that. We have to talk, Laura. Not now because Jeremiah needs our full attention, but as soon as he's better we're going to sit down and discuss some things. Important things."

"I…" Laura started, frowning in confusion.

Before she could continue a knock sounded at the cabin door. John got to his feet and crossed the room to open the door. Mitch stepped quickly into the room.

"Close the door," Mitch said, keeping his voice low. "You don't want a draft on Jeremiah. How's he doing?"

"He'll be fine," Laura said. "He has a little cold and will require some tender loving care."

"Well, he's in the right place to get it," Mitch said, smiling.

"Yep," John said.

Mitch shifted his attention to his brother. "Listen, John, your other two sisters, Katherine and Serena, are on the telephone up at the house. They got the idea to place a conference call from Wynborough on the chance they could speak with you. They can't get away right now to come meet you, but they figured they could at least say hello."

"I can't leave Jeremiah," John said.

"Oh, heavens, John, go talk to Serena and Katherine," Laura said, smiling. "How clever of them to think of putting together a conference call. It will be fun, John. You will have met all four of your sisters then."

"Well..."

"I'll just sit here and hold Jeremiah." Laura laughed. "With the mood he's in, I imagine he'll go off like an air raid siren if I try to put him in his crib before he falls asleep."

John hesitated, then nodded. A few minutes later he and Mitch left the cabin.

Laura watched them go, then shifted her gaze to Jeremiah, who was beginning to nod off to sleep.

What *important* things did John want to discuss with her? she wondered. Oh, surely he wasn't going to suggest that they continue their affair. He wouldn't take advantage of her vulnerability, the knowledge that she'd lost her heart to him.

No, John wouldn't do that.

Would he?

Laura sighed.

She was in love with John Colton, but she didn't for one minute think she understood what made him tick. That kind of *knowing* came to couples over time, people who were together day in, day out, in a committed relationship.

A rainbow wish togetherness.

And that was something she would never have with John.

John hunched into his jacket and shoved his hands into his pockets as he trudged back to the cabin in the cold night air.

Strange, he thought. He'd been on the telephone with Serena and Katherine, plus their husbands, for over an hour. The conversation had flowed easily, with no uncomfortable silences. Just as with Alexandra and Elizabeth, he felt as though he'd known Serena and Katherine for years.

The four princesses...his sisters...were down-to-earth, open and warm. None of them was pressuring him to embrace his identity as Prince James Wyndham of Wynborough. They simply expressed heart-felt joy that he was alive.

Whenever he thought of the horror his birth parents had experienced all those years ago, he immediately centered on Jeremiah and how he would feel if something happened to his son. The mere image of it in his mind made his blood run cold and a painful knot tighten in his gut. He could understand his birth parents' need to see him—their son—yet they were still holding back, allowing him time and space to come to grips with his newfound identity. The queen and king were a class act, no doubt about it.

John quickened his step as the cabin came into view, visible in the silvery glow of the moon and the millions of stars in the heavens.

Laura and Jeremiah were waiting for him in that little house. The woman and the boy he loved beyond measure.

His family.

A smile broke across John's face and he began to run, eager to close the distance separating him from Laura and Jeremiah.

Jeremiah was surely in his crib asleep by now, he thought, so this was it. He was going to tell Laura that he loved her. He was going to ask Laura to be his wife.

He was going to humbly request that Laura Bishop allow him to share her rainbow wish... forever.

Chapter Twelve

John entered the cabin, then frowned as he closed the door quietly behind him, a wave of disappointment sweeping through him.

Laura was curled up in the corner of the sofa asleep, her head resting on a throw pillow.

John shrugged out of his jacket and set it on a chair with his Stetson. He walked quickly down the hall to check on a peacefully sleeping Jeremiah, then returned to the living room.

He stood next to the sofa, gazing at Laura, visible in the glow of the firelight, filling his senses with the very sight of her.

He loved this woman, he thought incredulously. As unbelievable as it still seemed to him, he was truly and deeply in love with Laura.

He wanted to kiss her awake, to declare his love, to ask her to marry him. He wanted to seal their commitment to a future together with a kiss, then make sweet, slow love to her through the hours of the night.

But, no, that wasn't fair. Laura wouldn't have fallen asleep if she wasn't tired. He'd waited a lifetime for this moment, not even realizing for so many years what had been missing from his existence. He would just have to be patient a while longer, then he'd pour out his heart to Laura.

He retrieved a blanket from the bedroom, removed Laura's shoes, then tucked the blanket around her. Leaning over, he kissed her on the forehead.

"Sleep well, my love," he whispered.

He added another log to the fire, then went to bed, eager to sleep the night away to bring the light of the new day.

"Dada," Jeremiah yelled. "Mama. Up. Up. Up. Dada-a-a."

John jerked upright on the bed, then flopped back onto the pillow in the next instant. He blinked, then flung away the blankets and reached on the floor for his jeans.

"Mama," Jeremiah hollered, then began to cry. "Da-a-a-da."

"Coming, sport," John muttered, pulling on and zipping his jeans.

He strode from the room, then stopped dead in

his tracks when he entered the living room. The blanket he'd placed over Laura the previous night was folded neatly on the sofa and her shoes were no longer on the floor. He looked at the door, the sofa, then frowned.

"Damn," he said, continuing on his way to Jeremiah's room.

Two hours later, Jeremiah had been dressed, fed and the kitchen set to rights. John bundled the baby into his jacket and mittens, put on his own coat and Stetson and headed for the main house in search of Laura.

When he stepped into the kitchen, Betty turned from the stove.

"I was just going to come get you," she said.

"Oh?" John said, smiling. "Did you make some cinnamon rolls?"

"No," Betty said, not returning his smile. "You have company this morning."

"Again?" John said, raising his eyebrows. "Who is it? I've spoke to all four of my sisters."

"Yes, I know you have," Betty said. "In fact, Elizabeth and Rafe left for home an hour ago. They said to tell you that they'd talk to you again soon."

"Then who's here to see me?" John said.

"It's the Reverend Harold Tucker and his wife, Lucy, from town. Reverend Tucker said it was imperative that they speak with you."

"Why? What for? I only vaguely remember who they are. It's been years since I've seen them. Well,

I did bump into them in town since I've been back, but they acted strange...I don't know...like they were uncomfortable being near me. Why would they show up here?''

''I have no idea what they want with you,'' Betty said, ''but Lucy is pale as a ghost, so it must be something important. You best go see what's on their minds. Give me Jeremiah.''

John handed over the baby, then removed his own coat and Stetson, placing them on a chair by the table. A strange and chilling sense of foreboding suffused him as he left the kitchen.

John entered the living room at the same moment that Laura appeared from the hallway. The man and woman who had been sitting on the sofa got to their feet quickly, their eyes darting back and forth between John and Laura.

Oh, darn, Laura thought. What terrible timing she had. She had hurried from the cabin before John was awake so she wouldn't have to see him. She'd thought everything through, and come to the conclusion that John was going to propose that they continue their affair. No strings. No commitments. Just keep on...keeping on.

There was no other conclusion she could come to. She knew his stand on raising Jeremiah alone, had heard him say that Jeremiah was his and no one else's.

She just couldn't bear to hear John say that he wanted her only as his mistress for heaven only knew how long.

So what did she do? She'd walked into the living room at the exact moment that John did. Well, thank goodness he had company waiting to see him. She could make her escape. No problem.

Laura was brought back to attention as John made introductions. She said all the required "Pleased to meet yous" as she inched her way toward the door leading to the kitchen. "I'll leave you folks to chat," she said, producing a small smile.

"Yes, thank you," Reverend Tucker said. "I think it best that we speak with John privately."

"Whatever you've come to talk to me about can be said in Laura's presence," John said. "Let's all sit down, shall we?"

"That's not necessary, John," Laura said. "This is obviously a private conversation."

"Stay," he said. "Please."

Oh, good grief, Laura thought. John knew she wouldn't cause a scene in front of strangers.

"Yes, all right," she said, sighing.

She sat down on a love seat facing the sofa where the Tuckers were once again perched, her eyes widening for a moment as John settled onto the cushion next to her.

"Except for those quick hellos in town," John said to the Tuckers, "it's been a long time since I've seen you both."

"Yes," Harold Tucker said. "Yes, it has." He cleared his throat. "John, only very recently did Lucy unburden her soul to me regarding an incident that took place years before I met and married her.

"I convinced her that the proper thing to do was for her to come here to The Rocking C, tell you her story and ask for your forgiveness."

"I don't understand," John said. "My forgiveness? I don't think Lucy and I have exchanged more than a dozen words in the past years. How could she have offended me in any way?"

"It wasn't something she said," Harold said. "It was what she did." He looked at his wife and patted her hand gently. "Lucy? The time has come, my dear. Be strong. Gather your courage."

Heavens, Laura thought, that poor woman looked as if she was going to shatter into a million pieces. She was so pale and she was twisting a handkerchief between her trembling hands. What on earth was she about to confess to John?

Lucy Tucker drew a shuddering breath, then looked directly at John.

"Please, let me start at the beginning," the woman said, her voice quivering. "I was the product of a broken home. My mother died when I was sixteen, and I set out on my own, fiercely determined to have the kind of life I'd always dreamed about.

"But I was so young, inexperienced, vulnerable, and I became involved with a man named Roy Hanes. We...we moved through the Southwest, committing small crimes, staying one step ahead of the authorities.

"Then Roy decided to make the big time, as he put it," Lucy went on. "He...he kidnapped a baby, James Wyndham. He kidnapped *you,* John."

"What?" John said, leaning forward. "You were involved in my kidnapping?"

Lucy nodded, then sniffled. "Yes. Yes, I was. But you must believe me when I say I didn't have a choice." Lucy shuddered. "I realized very quickly that it had been a horrible thing to do. I took the baby—took you—and ran away from Roy in the dead of night.

"Then I learned of the fire that killed Roy, and how everyone believed you were dead. I was so afraid. I didn't think anyone would believe my story. I kept thinking I'd be sent to prison and my dreams would die. Then I'd be as good as dead."

"My God," John whispered.

"I tried to care for you, but it wasn't long before I had to admit to myself that I couldn't take care of a baby," Lucy said, tears spilling onto her pale cheeks. "I couldn't make enough money to feed you, buy you clothes, provide you with a decent place to live.

"So I wrapped you in the blanket we'd snatched up when we took you, and I left you on the doorstep of The Sunshine Home for Children in my hometown of Hope, Arizona. The Colton family adopted you later."

John lunged to his feet. "Why didn't you come forward and tell everyone that the baby was James Wyndham? Didn't you give even a moment's thought to the agony the parents of that baby—*my* parents—were going through? They thought I was dead, Lucy. Their hearts were broken. How could you keep silent?''

''I was terribly frightened,'' Lucy said, a sob catching in her throat. ''I really believed I would be sent to prison for the rest of my life. I watched you grow up as John Colton. You were happy, healthy, had a loving family. In my mind I believed I'd done the right thing by you. But I know now that I was wrong. Unforgivably wrong.''

''The right thing?'' John yelled. ''You allowed people to suffer needlessly. Gabriella and Phillip Wyndham believed their son was dead.''

''I'm sorry, so very sorry.'' Lucy covered her face with her hands and wept.

''John,'' Laura said, ''please sit down. I realize this has all come as a shock to you, but Lucy has carried this burden within her for so many years. She's asking you to forgive her. She was so young, John. Young, and foolish, and frightened. What's done, is done. It's time to look to the future, not harbor bitterness about the past. Please, John.''

John dragged one hand through his hair, then sank back onto the love seat with a sigh. He shook his head and stared up at the ceiling for a long moment before looking at Lucy again.

''You're right, Laura. Focusing on the past isn't going to serve any purpose.'' John paused. ''Lucy, you were just a kid when all this happened. I give you credit for saving me from Roy...and the fire, and for having the courage to come here today to tell the truth. If you've come for forgiveness, then know you have it. I don't want to live my life in the past or dwell on things neither of us can change. Well, thank you for coming.''

''Bless you, John,'' Reverend Tucker said.

John and the Tuckers got to their feet and John followed them to the front door.

A chill swept through Laura as she watched the trio cross the room.

Something was terribly wrong, she thought. John had erupted in anger upon hearing Lucy's confession, which was very understandable.

And now? What was he thinking? What was he feeling?

John closed the door behind the Tuckers, then turned slowly and looked at Laura. She stared at him intently, unable to decipher the expression on his face.

''John?'' she said tentatively. ''Are…are you all right?''

He laughed, the sound a sharp, rough-edged noise that held no trace of real humor.

''Yeah, sure,'' he said gruffly. ''I'm dandy, really super. I just sat in a room with the woman who was instrumental in the devastation of my birth parents, and the stripping away of my identity.'' He shook his head. ''Hell.''

Laura got to her feet and went to stand in front of John.

''That's all in the past, John, just like you said. What's important is the present and future. You have Jeremiah now, as well as sisters, brothers-in-law and another set of parents.

"You told Lucy that you forgave her for what she did. You meant that, didn't you?"

"Yeah. What's done is done. Old news, I guess," John said gruffly.

"Yes, and now you have the luxury of having options as to where you want to raise your son, and what career you wish to pursue. You are in many ways a very fortunate man."

"Nice speech, Laura," he said, frowning. "Except you left out a big piece from the pretty little picture you just painted."

"What piece?" she said, matching his frown.

"Who in the hell am I?" he said, nearly shouting.

"Well, you are..." Laura's voice trailed off.

"Gotcha, sweetheart. You don't know, either."

"But—"

"No." John sliced one hand through the air. "I've been fooling myself, thinking that I was actually accepting all of this, getting a handle on it. What a joke."

John moved around Laura and began to pace.

"I've mixed up both of my identities, both of my worlds, stirred them into a pot and just took out what suited me, what fit, was comfortable. I hid in that cabin with my son and actually convinced myself that I could have it all, be truly happy for the first time in my life."

He stopped and met Laura's gaze again. Her

breath caught as she saw the raw pain in John's eyes and etched on his face.

She wanted to go to him, to wrap her arms around him, to tell him he wasn't alone in his confusion and upset. Tell him she was there for him, would help him find the missing piece to the picture.

Tell him that she loved him and would stay by his side forever.

It didn't matter if he was John Colton or James Wyndham. She was in love with the man he was.

Tears closed Laura's throat and she said nothing. Nothing at all.

"John," Betty said, coming into the living room. "Jeremiah went to sleep. I put him on one of the beds with pillows around him so he won't roll off."

John nodded. "Okay. Thanks. I'm going to go tell Mitch what happened here with the Tuckers so he and Alex can share the details with Gabriella and Phillip."

"What *did* happen with the Tuckers?" Betty said.

"Laura will bring you up to date," he said. "After I talk to Mitch, I'm going for a walk. I need to be alone for a while. I'll be back to get Jeremiah."

Betty nodded as John strode from the room.

"Gracious," Betty said, looking at Laura. "John is so tense, he's crackling, could probably start a brush fire by walking across a field."

"He's extremely upset," Laura said quietly.

"What in the blue blazes did that Lucy Tucker say to him?"

Laura sighed. "I'll tell you her story, but that's

not what is really bothering John. He just... Oh, Betty, he's so confused. He doesn't know who he is.''

''I see,'' Betty said slowly. ''Well, he won't find any peace within himself, any happiness, until he discovers the answer.'' She shook her head. ''I can only imagine how unsettling it would be to suddenly be told you're not who you thought you'd been for thirty years. Poor John.''

''Or is it 'poor James?''' Laura said.

''You're right. My stars, what a dilemma. The thing is, the conclusions that John comes to, the decisions he makes, will have a profound effect on Jeremiah. As he looks to the future, he has a son to consider, as well as himself.''

But not a wife, Laura thought dismally. No, there was no wife in that unknown future of John's. Whichever identity he chose to claim, whatever world he existed in, he would do it only with Jeremiah. Just the two of them.

She would be on the outside looking in, like a child with her nose pressed to the window of a candy store she wasn't allowed to enter.

''Laura?'' Betty said. ''Are you all right, honey? You look a tad upset yourself.''

''I'm fine.'' Laura smiled faintly. ''I'll tell you what Lucy Tucker disclosed, then I'll go sit by Jeremiah so he won't be frightened if he wakes up and finds that he's not in his own crib.''

''You love that baby, don't you?''

''Yes,'' Laura whispered. And she loved that

baby's father, always would. "Yes, I do. I love Jeremiah very, very much."

John walked across the land of The Rocking C with no particular destination in mind. He simply put one foot in front of the other as he struggled to quiet the cacophony of voices in his head.

John Colton? James Wyndham? The Rocking C? Wynborough? Jeremiah Colton? Jeremiah Wyndham?

And what about Laura? he asked himself.

"I, John James Colton Wyndham, take thee, Laura Bishop..."

With a snort of disgust, John shook his head.

Talk about a fantasy. How in the hell did he think he could make Laura happy when he didn't even know who he was, what it would take to make *himself* happy?

There it was. Bottom line.

He had no right to declare his love to Laura, to ask her to marry him, because he wasn't free to do that. He was held captive in a maze of confusion and doubts, not even close to knowing what to do, what road to take, what identity to claim, what world to exist in.

He was a mental and emotional mess, and no one could help him find the answers he so desperately needed.

He was alone.

Just as he'd always been.

John settled onto a large rock and stared at the land that stretched to the horizon.

The Rocking C, he thought. He'd never fit in here, didn't belong on this spread. He wasn't a rancher, a true Colton.

Would it be more honest and honorable to step up and announce that he didn't deserve to carry the Colton name and was, therefore, going to be James Wyndham?

Prince James Wyndham?

''Hell,'' he said aloud. ''I'm closer to being a frog than a prince.''

He ran one hand across his face, then sighed; a sigh that came from the very depths of his troubled soul. Exhaustion swept over him like a crushing weight, making it difficult to breathe in, then out.

By sheer force of will, John blanked his mind and just sat on the rock in the midst of the vast land.

Alone.

Laura did not have an opportunity to speak privately with John during the next three days.

Each morning, she watched out the kitchen window as John brought Jeremiah up from the cabin to one of the corrals where Mitch, or a ranch hand, would take the baby for a slow horse ride around the inside of the enclosure.

In the evenings, John and Jeremiah joined everyone for dinner in the main house. Laura was acutely and painfully aware that John never looked directly at her during the meal, nor asked her any questions that would require her to speak to him.

It was apparent from John's haggard appearance that he wasn't sleeping well. He was also extremely preoccupied, often requiring something to be repeated before he could comment.

The minute that dinner was over, John scooped Jeremiah from his high chair, mumbled ''thanks'' and ''good night,'' and returned to the cabin with his son.

Mid-morning of the fourth day since the Tuckers had visited The Rocking C, Laura was sitting in the living room reading a book by the fire when John suddenly appeared.

''Laura?'' He walked slowly toward her, stopping next to her chair.

Laura looked up at him. ''Hello, John.''

''Are you busy? I thought we could go into town and get the stuff for Jeremiah's birthday party. Tomorrow is his big day. Alex is out by the corral where Jeremiah is having his ride on a horse. Alex said she'd baby-sit Jeremiah while we're gone.''

''Yes, fine. I'll go into town with you.''

Laura placed a slip of paper in the book, closed it and got to her feet. She put the book in the chair, then moved around John.

''I'll get my coat and purse,'' she said. ''I'll be right back.''

''How are you?'' John said when Laura was halfway across the room.

She stopped and turned to meet his gaze.

"I'm...all right," she said, unable to produce even a small smile. "And you? You look very tired, John."

"Yeah, well, I haven't been sleeping much. I have a great deal on my mind. I feel like one of those hamsters, just chasing my thoughts around and around, not really getting anywhere, not finding any answers."

Laura wrapped her trembling hands over her elbows, her heart aching as she heard John's weary, defeated tone.

"I'm so sorry," she said softly, "that you're going through this turmoil. I wish I had a magic wand I could wave to give you the answers you're seeking."

"There you go," he said, smiling slightly. "We'll check out the stores in Hope and see if there's a magic wand anywhere."

"Okay," Laura said, smiling.

"Look," he said, "I'm going to try like hell to leave my troubles here on The Rocking C as we drive away. Shopping for Jeremiah's birthday party should be fun, and I sure could use a dose of fun. Deal?"

Laura nodded. "Deal."

And it *was* fun.

Laura fully expected that her cheeks would start to ache from the constant smile on her face. True to his word, John seemed to shed his worries and woes like removing a heavy, uncomfortable cloak. His smile and laughter were real and rich, and genuine merriment danced in the depths of his blue eyes.

"Clowns," he declared, as they entered the first store. "A party needs a theme, and we'll have happy, bright-colored clowns."

"Great," Laura said. "Okay, let's see. We need a paper tablecloth, plates, cups—"

"Balloons," John added. "You get the paper stuff and I'll go check out the balloons."

Laura laughed. "Just remember that the number of balloons you buy is the same number you have to blow up."

"No problem. I'll snag Mitch to help me. He's full of hot air half of the time anyway."

When Laura reached the checkout counter with the paper supplies, John was holding a sack in one hand.

"You already bought the balloons?" she said. "Wouldn't it have been easier to purchase everything at once?"

John shrugged.

"Did you get balloons to match the colors of these clowns on the paper goods?" Laura said.

"I...um...I got the ones I wanted," he said, not looking directly at her.

"Okay. Whatever," she said, frowning slightly in confusion.

"Let's go. Let's go," John said, waving one hand toward the cashier.

"What's the rush?"

''The toy store is calling my name, sweet Laura.''

''Oh, I see,'' she said, laughing in delight.

The toy store was small, but definitely had enough to offer to please John. Laura trekked behind him as he went down every aisle, examining the display.

He selected a shiny red fire truck that made a noise like a siren when a button was pushed, an inflated clown that popped back up when it was pushed over, a jack-in-the-box and a blue ball that was bigger than the red one Jeremiah now had.

Laura chose a soft, cuddly teddy bear that played a lullaby when a knob was turned.

When the purchases were locked in the car, they settled into a red vinyl booth in Ruby's Diner for lunch. They were soon consuming hamburgers, fries and thick milkshakes.

''Delicious,'' Laura said.

''This place has been here forever,'' John said, glancing around. ''I don't think they've changed one thing in here since they went into business.'' He looked at two cowboys who slid onto stools at the counter opposite where he and Laura were sitting. ''It's a popular spot to eat.''

''With just cause,'' Laura said. ''This is one of the best hamburgers I've ever had.''

''Hey, Butch, did you hear the news?'' one of the cowboys said to the other. ''Mitch Colton up and married himself some fancy-pants princess.''

John stiffened and narrowed his eyes, staring at the backs of the two men. Laura looked quickly at the ranch hands, then back at John.

"Yeah, I heard," Butch said. "He brought her to The Rocking C. Cripe, Mack, what's a prissy princess going to do with herself all day on a working ranch? Serve tea and crumpets to the hands or something?"

Mack said, "I bet she's ugly as sin but has bucks, and Mitch married her for her money. That makes sense. Hell, once you turn out the lights, it doesn't matter what she looks like if her bank account is big enough."

"That's it," John muttered. "They're done."

"John, don't," Laura said anxiously.

John slid out of the booth.

"Oh, dear heaven," Laura whispered.

John closed the distance separating him from the two men and tapped each on the shoulder. They spun around on their stools and looked up at him.

"Yeah? What?" Butch said.

"Know who I am?" John said gruffly.

"Nope, but you're bothering me. Buzz off."

"The name is Colton," John said. "John Colton of The Rocking C."

"Oh, hell," Mack said. "Mitch's brother."

"Got it in one," John said, nodding. "You boys have had a lot to say about Mitch, and I didn't like what I was hearing. Not one little bit."

"Hey, man," Butch said, raising both hands, "we didn't mean anything by it. It's just news, you know what I mean? Mitch marrying a princess and all? I apologize if we said anything unfitting about your brother."

"*And* my sister," John said, his voice laced with anger.

"Huh?"

"You're in double trouble with your big mouths," John said. "Mitch Colton is my brother. His wife is my sister. You don't have to understand it, just believe it. Nobody talks that way about my family."

"No problem," Butch said, inching off the stool. "I apologize twice. Two times. You bet. Once for what I said about your brother, and another for your sister. Stay cool. We're gone. Come on, Mack. Let's get out of here right now."

"Real sorry, Mr. Colton," Mack said, sliding past John. "Didn't mean any harm. No, sir, surely didn't. No, sir. 'Bye."

John watched the pair nearly run out of the diner, then slowly straightened the fingers that he'd curled into fists at his sides. He returned to the booth and sat down across from Laura again.

"Well," she said, taking a steadying breath, "that was...interesting."

"It was necessary," John said, meeting her gaze.

"Oh, I thoroughly agree," she said quickly. "The *interesting* part was what you said to those two men."

John frowned. "What do you mean?"

Laura reached over and placed a hand on one of John's on the top of the table.

"You said that you were John Colton of The Rocking C," she said gently. "You said that Mitch was your brother and his wife was your sister. You said that nobody could talk the way they had about your family.''

She paused, tightening her hold on John's hand.

''Oh, John, don't you see? Deep down inside, you do know exactly who you are.''

Chapter Thirteen

The sense of elation that consumed John as he heard what Laura said evaporated seconds later, causing him to knit his brows.

"No," he said with a sigh, "that's not true. I still don't know who I *really* am, Laura. What I said to those two jerks was just more of the same. I'm taking a little from one of my worlds, some from the other—whatever suits me at the moment. That's not realistic. I have to choose one over the other, and I hit a brick wall every time I attempt to reach some concrete decisions."

"But—"

"Enough of this topic. This trip to town is all about fun, remember? Did you get paper, bows and tape, so we can wrap Jeremiah's gifts? I wasn't paying attention to what all you had at the checkout in that store.''

''Yes, I bought all that,'' she said. ''I have everything we need.''

Except the answers that John was so desperately seeking, she thought. She could use several answers for herself as well.

Such as how was she going to embrace a future without John and Jeremiah in it? How was she going to cope with the heartache and loneliness? How would she stop the tears from flowing during the long, dark hours of the endless nights ahead?

''We have to go to the bakery,'' John said, bringing Laura from her gloomy thoughts.

''Why? I thought Betty agreed to bake Jeremiah's birthday cake.''

''She did, but she said they sell plastic figures at the bakery to put on the top of cakes. You know, animals, brides and grooms, that sort of stuff. I sure hope they have clowns.''

''I'm...sure they will,'' Laura said quietly. ''Clowns are very popular.''

Bride and groom figures, she thought, for the top of a wedding cake. A cake for the reception after two people in love had exchanged sacred vows to stay together until death parted them. A cake that was visible evidence of a rainbow wish that had come true.

Laura sighed and John looked at her questioningly.

''What's wrong?'' he said.

"Oh...nothing. I'm full, can't eat another bite, that's all."

"That's too bad," he said. "They have terrific homemade pie here."

Laura laughed. "I'll watch you enjoy a piece. I'm stuffed."

"I'll give you a bite if you change your mind," John said, smiling. "What's mine is yours, ma'am."

Except for his heart, Laura thought dismally.

During the return drive to The Rocking C, Laura felt as though she could actually see John putting the walls firmly back into place around him.

He was once again shutting her out, concentrating solely on the momentous decisions he was facing.

She could, she supposed, break the oppressive silence in the car by asking John what the important issue was that he had wanted to discuss with her. But, no, that would be a foolish, masochistic thing to do. She was convinced he wanted to propose that they continue their affair if he chose to raise Jeremiah in Wynborough.

And if he elected to stay on The Rocking C? Oh, well, Laura, it had been great, but see you.

No, she wouldn't put herself through that, wouldn't take part in that discussion. She knew the chilling truth already, certainly didn't need to hear it all spelled out for her.

John parked in front of the ranch house and turned off the ignition.

"I'll get everything out of the car later," he said,

staring out the front window of the vehicle. "I can wrap Jeremiah's gifts after he goes to bed tonight. I appreciate your going into town with me."

"I enjoyed it," Laura said quietly, reaching for the handle on the door.

"Laura."

She looked over at him. "Yes?"

"I...I just want you to know," he said, meeting her gaze, "that I wish things were different, weren't such a muddled mess and...Laura, I..." *I love you so damn much.* "Thanks."

Laura nodded, then got out of the car and hurried into the house.

John watched her until she disappeared from view, then smacked the steering wheel with the palm of one hand so hard, a stinging pain shot up his arm.

"Damn it," he said, shaking his hand.

The birthday party was scheduled for lunchtime the next day.

Just before noon, Laura sat on the edge of her bed, the door to her room open enough that she could hear the laughing and talking that floated down the hallway.

She sighed and closed her eyes for a moment, reaching deep within herself for the fortitude to join in the festivities with a bright smile on her face while her heart was breaking.

Jeremiah was one year old today, she thought. Where would he be when he turned two? Then three? Four? Where would John have chosen to raise his son?

Raise his son *alone.*

Or maybe not alone at some point in the future. John might very well fall in love and marry, have a wife, a mother for Jeremiah, create more children with that woman. There was also the possibility that John Colton might choose to be James Wyndham. Or maybe he'd—

Oh, Laura, stop, she admonished herself, pressing her fingertips to her throbbing temples. Why was she traveling down that mental road, being so cruel to herself with her own thoughts?

Enough of this. She had a birthday party to attend for a little boy she loved as though he was her own son.

''Smile,'' she said, getting to her feet. ''Even if it kills you...smile.''

She straightened the waistband of the red sweater she wore over gray slacks, lifted her chin and marched from the room.

When she entered the dining room, the smile that lit up her face was genuine as she was caught up immediately in the festive mood.

Happy clowns pranced around the border of the tablecloth that was spread over the long table, and a three-layer cake with plastic clowns on top had the place of honor in the center of the table.

John had dressed Jeremiah in red overalls and a red-and-white striped, long-sleeved shirt. The baby was toddling around the room, a party hat perched on his head. The brightly wrapped gifts were on top of the buffet against the wall.

John was wearing a long-sleeved, dark blue Western shirt with jeans, and Laura's party frame of mind vanished as she drank in the sight of his broad shoulders, his long, muscular legs, and his rugged features that boasted a big smile as he talked to Mitch.

Alexandra was placing napkins and plates on the table as Betty bustled into the room carrying a huge platter of sandwiches.

"Sandwiches, potato chips, salad, drinks," Betty said, surveying the table. "All I need is Jeremiah's lunch and we're ready to roll. I'll be right back."

"But where are the balloons?" Laura said, forcing a lightness to her voice as Betty left the room. "Don't tell me that you and Mitch didn't have enough oomph to blow them up, John."

Everyone stopped what they were doing and looked at Laura.

"Mama." Jeremiah walked to where Laura stood and flung himself at her legs. She picked him up and he patted her nose. "Mama."

"Hello, birthday boy," she said, then kissed him on the cheek. She smiled at John again. "Well? The balloons? I'm waiting to hear the excuses for why they aren't here, gentlemen."

"I blew them up, all of them," John said quietly.

Laura laughed. "And they flew away?"

Jeremiah wiggled to get down and Laura set him on his feet. Betty returned with the baby's lunch.

"Party time," the housekeeper said. "Everyone

sit. Come on, Jeremiah, I'll put you in your high chair right at the head of the table.''

"I'll get the balloons," John said.

As John left the room, Laura settled onto a chair and smiled across the table at Alex. Jeremiah pounded merrily on the high chair tray as Betty sat down next to Laura.

"This is good practice for you, Alex," Laura said. "You'll be an expert at baby birthday parties by the time you need to put them on for your little one."

Alex laughed. "I've already discovered who the child will be at those parties. Mitch wanted to start this event an hour ago."

"Well, hey," Mitch said, sitting down next to Alex, "why wait an entire morning on the big day? We'll have breakfast birthday parties for our kids."

"Kids? Plural?" Alex paused, then nodded. "Well, sure, all right, as long as they arrive on the scene one at a time."

"Okay," Mitch said. "One...two...three...four..."

"Whoa," Alex said, laughing.

"Whoa," Jeremiah yelled. "Whoa. Whoa."

"Thank you, Jeremiah," Alex said. "I appreciate your support. I... Oh, my, look at those beautiful balloons. Such lovely pastel colors, just like a—"

"Rainbow," Laura said, her voice hushed and her heart seeming to skip a beat.

John hesitated, then walked slowly forward, his arms filled with large balloons that had long, matching silky ribbons attached. He stopped by Laura's chair and looked directly into her eyes.

"You truly deserve to have your rainbow," he said quietly. "I know that balloons don't fulfill the wish, but this is the only rainbow I can offer you, Laura. I just wanted you to know that I hadn't forgotten about your rainbow wish. They're yours, all yours. They belong to you...both the rainbow and the wish."

"Rainbow wish?" Mitch whispered to Alex.

"Shh," Alex said. "I don't know what it means, either, but it's obviously something very special."

"Yeah, well..." John cleared his throat and extended the balloons toward Laura. "Here."

Laura got to her feet, acutely aware that her knees were trembling and her eyes were brimming with tears. She accepted the bouquet of balloons from John.

"Thank you," she said softly. *I love you so much, John.* What a bittersweet gift this was from the rough, tough, yet sensitive and caring man who had stolen her heart for all time. And that stolen heart was shattering, because John was making it clear that he would not be a part of her rainbow wish. Not ever. "Thank you for being so thoughtful and...and honest."

They continued to gaze into each other's eyes and the room faded into oblivion. There was just the two of them and a rainbow.

"Whoa. Whoa," Jeremiah shouted.

Laura and John jerked at the sudden noise and the spell was broken.

Laura struggled to regain her composure as she nestled the balloons onto one of the empty chairs at the table.

John sat down next to Jeremiah and began to feed the birthday boy his lunch.

The party had officially begun.

Hours later, when the festivities had ended and everyone turned in for the night, Laura placed her balloons on the floor next to her bed and fell asleep with one hand resting on the bouquet, her dreams replete with her rainbow wish...and John.

When she awoke the next morning, all the air had sifted out of the balloons, turning them into a flat puddle of color. Laura buried her face in her pillow and wept for much more than the loss of her precious gift.

After breakfast John sat on the floor in the cabin with Jeremiah, who was busily moving from one treasure to the next, thoroughly enjoying his birthday gifts.

"So, how did you like your party yesterday, sport?" John said. "You made out like a bandit. What a bunch of stuff you got. Toys, toys, toys."

"Toys," Jeremiah said, throwing his new ball across the room.

"Go for it," John said, then leaned his back against the sofa.

Yep, he thought. Jeremiah had had quite a party

to celebrate his first birthday. There had been clowns galore, cake, presents and…balloons.

John dragged his hands down his face and sighed. Balloons. Rainbow-colored balloons.

When he'd been in the store in Hope, he'd had every intention of buying bright, primary-colored balloons to match the clown decorations.

But then he'd seen the pastel balloons, had been drawn to them as though an invisible magnet was pulling him forward.

It had suddenly been so important that Laura know that he'd really listened to her on the night they'd met, that he'd remembered every word she'd said, what she had shared with him about her rainbow wish.

He loved her so deeply, so intensely, he'd never be able to describe the depth of that love.

If his circumstances were different, they could have it all—marriage, a home, Jeremiah and more babies they would create by beautiful lovemaking.

They could have, together, Laura's rainbow wish…forever.

But his life was a mess, his confusion all-consuming. Laura would never know how he felt about her. He couldn't make her happy, because he didn't even know where he belonged, or who he truly was.

He might never know.

So, he'd presented Laura with the bouquet of balloons, given back her secret wish, set her free to find a man who would be all that she needed and wanted in her life's partner.

Man, he hated this.

The thought of another man touching Laura, making love to her, gaining her trust and love for all time, caused a cold fist to tighten in his gut.

But he had no other choice than to walk away from Laura Bishop.

He would raise his son alone. Somewhere. He would decide, hopefully, at some point in the blurry future whether he and Jeremiah should have the last name of Colton, or Wyndham.

He had to find the answers he was so desperately seeking before he went straight out of his mind.

But as he struggled for inner peace and resolution, Laura would move forward with her life. Laura would be gone, but never, *never* forgotten.

"Hell," John said gruffly.

"Hell," Jeremiah said merrily, pushing his fire truck across the floor.

"You didn't hear that," John said. "Don't say 'hell,' Jeremiah."

"Hell, hell, hell," the baby echoed.

"Cripe," John said, shaking his head. "Jeremiah, say 'dada.'"

"Mama. Ma-a-ma."

"No," John said with a weary sigh. "Mama isn't going to be with us. It's just you and me, kiddo. All I have to do is figure out who we are and where we're going to live. Piece of cake." He snorted in disgust. "Yeah, right."

A knock sounded at the door.

"It's open," John called. "Enter at your own risk."

Alex entered the cabin.

"Is it dangerous in here?" she said, smiling. "Ah, so it is. You have an obstacle course of toys set up."

John got to his feet. "You'd better believe it. Jeremiah will run you down with his fire truck if you don't watch out." He paused. "What brings you to our castle, Princess Alex?"

"I came to see if Jeremiah is ready for his morning ride."

John frowned. "We usually don't do that until later."

"Yes, well, I… What I mean is, I could take him up now if it's all right. It won't disrupt his schedule, will it? It's fairly warm outside and… Okay?"

John studied Alex for a moment.

"Are you acting weird, or is it my imagination?" he said finally.

"Weird? Me?" she said, raising her eyebrows.

"Never mind. I'll change Jeremiah's diaper and put on his jacket. Jeremiah, do you want to go for a ride on a horse?"

Jeremiah clapped his hands. "Horse." He pushed himself up, teetered, then toddled toward Alex. "Horse."

"The vote is in," John said. "I might as well go with you two."

"No," Alex said quickly. "That is, why don't

you have some quiet time while you can? Just stay here in the cabin and relax. Yes, that's a great idea.''

John eyed her warily. "Yep, you're definitely acting weird."

Alex smiled at him sweetly.

A short while later, Alex and a jabbering Jeremiah left the cabin. John considered picking up the strewn toys, then decided it was a waste of energy since Jeremiah would redistribute them over the floor as soon as he was returned to the cabin.

John sank onto the sofa, then realized an instant later that he didn't have even a clue as to how to spend his idle time.

He sure as hell didn't feel like chasing his own thoughts around in the maddening circle in his mind. He wasn't even close to having the answers he needed.

He changed the sheet on Jeremiah's crib, wiped off the counters in the kitchen, added a few items to the grocery list held on the refrigerator with a magnet shaped like a cow, then wandered back into the living room.

A rap on the cabin door was a welcomed break in the oppressive silence within the walls of the small house, and John strode across the room to fling open the door.

He stared at the stranger standing before him, a distinguished, handsome man in his late fifties, who was wearing a perfectly tailored dark suit, white shirt and dark tie. He was tall, broad-shouldered, trim, had a full head of white hair and a neat white

beard and mustache. His blue eyes were riveted on
John.

"Hello," the man said, his voice strangely husky.
He cleared his throat and drew a deep breath, letting
it out slowly. "I'm sorry. This moment is rather
overwhelming. May I come in?"

John frowned. "That depends on who you are and
what you want."

"Yes, of course. I need to introduce myself.
I'm…King Phillip of Wynborough."

Chapter Fourteen

The world seemed to tilt on its axis for a moment, and John gripped the edge of the door tightly with one hand to steady himself.

"I realize that I've arrived on your doorstep with no warning," Phillip said, "and I hope you'll forgive Alexandra for her part in my duplicity, but I was afraid you might refuse to see me if you knew I was coming."

John shook his head slightly to clear away the strange buzzing noise in his ears.

"You thought I might refuse to see you?" he repeated. "Why?"

"May I come in?"

"Oh, yes, of course," John stepped back to allow Phillip to enter the cabin. "Sorry."

John closed the door, then turned to stare at Phillip Wyndham. Blue eyes met matching blue eyes for a long, heart-stopping moment.

"Please, sit down," John said, jerking his gaze from Phillip's. "Excuse the mess, but Jeremiah was playing with his birthday toys and... Why did you think I might refuse to see you?"

Phillip made his way through the scattered toys on the floor to sit on the chair by the fireplace. John sank onto the sofa, then leaned forward, resting his elbows on his knees and linking his fingers.

"I saw your son when Alexandra brought him up to the house," Phillip said, no hint of a smile on his face. "Your...that is, my wife, Gabriella, was holding Jeremiah when I left the house to come here to your cabin. She was crying and laughing at the same time. Jeremiah is the image of you as a baby."

John nodded, his gaze fixed on Phillip.

"You want an answer to your question," Phillip went on, "as to why I feared you might choose not to see me.

"I have been attempting to put myself in your place, to try to imagine how disturbing it has been for you to suddenly learn you're not who you've always believed yourself to be. That must be a terribly heavy emotional burden, a source of immeasurable confusion."

"Yes," John said, surprise evident in his voice.

"To come face to face with me would mean there would be nowhere to hide from your mental dilemma,'' Phillip said. ''But I'm afraid I put myself, my needs, selfishly first. I had to see you. I had to.''

''I understand,'' John said, nodding.

''When I introduced myself to you,'' Phillip said, ''I came very close to announcing 'I'm your father,' but I bit back those words, because I don't feel I have the right to say them.''

''What?'' John said, frowning.

''I'm also being extremely careful not to refer to you by name, not to call you James.'' Phillip shook his head. ''This is so very difficult.

''I want to touch you, hug you, hold you in my arms, see you smile, hear your laughter and... But I have to respect you and this—'' he swept one arm through the air ''—this distance between us.''

''Now I *don't* understand,'' John said, frowning and shaking his head.

''I saw you being born,'' Phillip said, his voice husky with emotion. ''I held you in my hands as you took your first deep breath, then wailed your displeasure over being so rudely removed from the safe haven of your...of Gabriella's womb.

''I walked the floor with you when you suffered through cutting your teeth, and swelled with pride as I watched you take your first steps.''

''You saw my first steps?'' John said, his entwined fingers tightening. ''I wondered if you did when Laura and I saw Jeremiah take his. It's because of Jeremiah that I came to realize the pain you suffered when I was kidnapped, then believed to be dead. I don't think I could handle it if something happened to Jeremiah.''

''The pain never really goes away. Oh, it diminishes in time, but it's always there, claiming a portion of your heart and soul.''

''Yes,'' John said quietly. ''I can believe that.''

''When I learned that you were alive,'' Phillip said, ''my first instinct was to rush here to The Rocking C, claim you as my son, tell you that it was time, at long last, to come home to us, where you belong.''

''But you didn't do that,'' John said.

''No. My role as your father ended shortly after you took those first wobbling steps of yours. You were snatched away, torn from my life, leaving an open, aching wound.

''I am not the one who taught you the values you took into adulthood. I wasn't there to soothe your fears as a young boy, stand by you during the turbulence of adolescence, watch as you walked away to find your place in the world as a man. Robert Colton did all those things for his son, John Colton. Robert is your father far more than I am.''

''But you gave me life,'' John said, his voice rising.

''Yes. Yes, I did, but Robert Colton gave you much, much more.''

''You're an incredible man,'' John said, awe ringing in his voice.

''No, I'm a simple man, who loves his son, has never stopped loving his son. I love you enough to make no demands of you, to walk out of your existence on this very day and never see you again, if that's what you want. I wish only for your happiness.''

''My happiness?'' John said. ''I can't find it inside of myself. *I don't know who I am anymore.* I don't know which of my worlds to choose, which identity fits. I'm torn in two. Can you understand that? Can you?

''I'm in love with a fantastic woman, with Laura, and I can't even tell her, because I'm not capable of making *her* happy if I can't...'' He shook his head. ''Hell.''

Phillip leaned forward, unconsciously mirroring John's pose.

''Why do you have to choose one world, one identity, over the other?'' Phillip said. ''Why can't you take what you want from each?''

John's eyes widened. ''What?''

''Raise your son on the island of Wynborough, if you so choose. Do it as John Colton, if that is who you wish to be. Or stay here on your Rocking C, but be James Wyndham and make Jeremiah a Wyndham. Oh, my beloved son, do whatever it takes to find inner peace and happiness, to have a future with the woman you love. Do it. Whatever is right for you. *Whatever will make you happy.*''

John lunged to his feet and dragged one hand through his hair.

''I don't believe this,'' he said, his voice raspy. ''That's what I've been doing...picking and choosing what I wanted. I kept telling myself that I was playing games, that it was wrong, a fantasy, that I really couldn't create a life, a future, that way.''

With agitated motions, John moved around the room, picking up Jeremiah's toys and placing them in the playpen. Phillip watched him with a concerned expression on his face.

''James...John,'' Phillip said finally, ''God knows that none of us asked for this nightmare, but it happened, was set into motion years and years ago. Now? Gabriella and I have pledged to count our blessings, to be grateful that you're alive, rather than harbor bitterness toward Lucy Tucker.''

John completed the chore he'd undertaken, only vaguely aware that he'd cleared the floor of toys. He turned to look at Phillip.

''As for you?'' Phillip went on. ''I truly believe that you've earned the right to do exactly as I stated. Gabriella and I will accept whatever decisions you make. From what I've learned about the Coltons, I'm certain they will do the same. We all love you...both of your families. You know that, don't you?''

Phillip got to his feet.

''Don't you, son?'' he said quietly.

A strange warmth suffused John, along with a foreign sense of inner peace like nothing he had ever known. It touched his heart, his mind, his very soul. An achy sensation gripped his throat and tears filled his eyes.

''Yes,'' he said hoarsely. ''Yes, I know that.

You...you gave me life thirty years ago, and you have just...given me my life...again.''

They moved at the same time, two men, the son and the father. They reached for each other, tears shimmering in matching blue eyes. Their embrace was powerful, not only in physical strength, but emotionally as well.

Years of pain, and loneliness, and heartache were pushed into oblivion as they savored the moment...along with dreams of the future.

Late that night, Laura parked in front of the ranch house and turned off the ignition to the car. She gripped the top of the steering wheel and rested her forehead on her hands, closing her eyes.

She was so tired, she thought, thoroughly exhausted, physically and mentally drained.

It was over. All of it. She couldn't stay on The Rocking C any longer, couldn't bear to be so close, yet so very, very far removed from John and Jeremiah.

The moment she'd seen Alexandra place Jeremiah in Queen Gabriella's loving arms, seen the baby pat his grandmother's nose, and witnessed Gabriella's heartfelt tears of joy, it had all come to an end for the outsider, social secretary Laura Bishop.

Laura raised her head and sighed, reliving in her mind the scene where she'd forced a smile onto her face and a light tone to her voice as she'd told Queen Gabriella and Alex that she was off to town for the day, was going to indulge in some quiet, private, lazy hours. They'd accepted her plans with no question, their attention riveted on Jeremiah.

The day had seemed endless as she'd wandered in and out of the stores in Hope. She'd eaten a lunch she didn't want at the diner, then continued on her aimless trek.

At one point in the late afternoon she'd thought she'd seen John across the street, then dismissed the idea in the next instant.

That would probably happen a great deal in the future, Laura thought bleakly. She'd be thinking of John, then imagine that she had actually seen him in a crowd of people beyond her reach. Always beyond her reach.

She'd finally gone to the movies and sat through the long film twice, unable to follow the story during either showing.

The final moment of truth had come at The Rocking C that morning when King Phillip had smiled warmly at Jeremiah, then said he was going to the cabin to see his son.

Queen Gabriella and King Phillip had exchanged a loving gaze, a brush of lips, then Phillip had squared his shoulders and left the house.

She knew, just somehow knew, that John and King Phillip would reach an understanding that would bring peace and happiness to them both. The Wyndhams and the Coltons were all part of John's family. They all loved him, whether he was John Colton or Prince James Wyndham of Wynborough.

They created a close-knit, loving circle that encompassed John and Jeremiah, leaving Laura on the outside looking in, her heart aching.

She just couldn't bear it any longer.

She would return to Wynborough tomorrow, as there was a great deal to do to prepare for the anniversary celebration of King Phillip's coronation.

"I have to leave here," Laura said aloud, struggling against threatening tears. "I have to. Now."

With the last ounce of energy she possessed, Laura got out of the car, trudged to the front door and entered the house.

The living room was dark, except for a small golden glow cast for several feet from the embers of the ebbing fire in the hearth. Laura closed the door with a quiet click and started across the room.

"Laura."

She gasped in shock at the sudden sound of her name and stopped in her tracks, her heart racing. A dark form rose from the sofa to stand with his back to the fire.

"John?" she said.

"Yes," he said quietly. "I've been waiting for you to come home."

What lovely words, Laura thought. *I've been waiting for you to come home.* But this wasn't her home, nor was John anticipating her arrival as her husband would in her rainbow wish.

"Why?" Laura said, keeping her voice low so as not to disturb the sleeping household. "What's wrong? Where's Jeremiah?"

"Betty is at the cabin with Jeremiah," John said.

"Could you come over here, please? I'd like to talk to you without waking everyone up."

Laura frowned, hesitated, then went around the sofa to stand in front of John. She looked up at him questioningly, able to see him clearly in the golden glow, but unable to decipher his expression.

"Would you take off your coat and sit down?" he said. "Please?"

"John, it's late and I'm very tired. Couldn't this keep until morning?"

"No," he said. "I've waited a lifetime and that's long enough."

"Pardon me?"

"Your coat?"

Laura removed her coat and placed it over the arm of the sofa, setting her purse on top. She fought the urge to fling herself into John's arms, then in the next moment wanted to run down the hall to the safety of her room.

She sank onto the middle cushion of the sofa and stared into the hearth. John added another log to the fire, then turned to look at Laura.

"Laura, I..." he started, then cleared his throat. "Hell, I've been sitting here for hours practicing what I was going to say to you, and I've forgotten every damn word." He paused, frowning. "Would you at least look at me?"

Laura clutched her hands tightly in her lap and shifted her gaze slowly to meet John's. The fresh log caught fire and the leaping flames brightened the room.

"I'm looking at you," she said.

"Right. You are. That's good." John cleared his throat again.

John was nervous, Laura thought incredulously. He was jumpy, edgy, and speaking in short, clipped sentences. What on earth was wrong with him?

"What on earth is wrong with you?" she said. "You're acting like someone who had been summoned to the principal's office or something. Could you sit down? I'm getting a crick in my neck from looking up at you."

"Oh, sure. You bet." John sat next to her, then shifted so he could face her. "I...um...I guess you know that Phillip Wyndham came to see me at the cabin this morning."

Laura nodded as she looked directly at him.

"Phillip is a hell of a fine man," John said. "I respect and admire him more than I can begin to tell you. Meeting him, talking to him, was very moving, very...emotional, for both of us."

"Yes," Laura said softly. "I'm sure it was."

"The thing is, Laura, that because of my conversation with Phillip, I have the answers I've been searching for so desperately. I am so grateful to him for showing me that I had those answers all along."

"I don't understand," Laura said, frowning.

"I was beating myself up, because I believed I was living in a fantasy," John went on. "I was picking what I wanted from the world of John Colton, and taking other things from the existence surrounding James Wyndham. Nice work if you can get it, I told myself, but not even close to reality.

"Where was my *real* happiness going to be found? Who in the hell was I? How could I even presume to think I could make someone else happy, if I couldn't get a grip on that emotion for myself? So many questions without answers. So damn many."

"But King Phillip showed you that you did have the answers?"

John reached over and covered Laura's entwined hands with one of his. He stretched his other arm across the top of the sofa and leaned toward her.

Oh, John, don't, Laura thought frantically. He was so close, so enticingly close. She could see the clear depths of his beautiful blue eyes, the late-hour stubble of beard on his rugged, handsome face. She could smell his aroma of fresh air, and wood smoke, and man.

His hand resting on hers was so strong, yet so gentle, and was causing a heated path to flash up her arms, across her breasts, then swirl and pulse low in her body.

John, don't do this to me.

"Laura," he said, his voice raspy, "Phillip enabled me to realize that I *can* pick and choose from both of my worlds, just as I was doing. I have the luxury of doing that because I've been blessed with two loving families, both of whom will accept me as I am, no matter what decisions I make regarding my future."

''Yes, I see,'' Laura said, nodding. ''That makes sense. It's wonderful...for both you and Jeremiah.''

''Hear me out, okay?''

''Yes.''

John took a deep breath, letting it out slowly.

''I'm going to take Jeremiah to Wynborough to raise him there. I'm going to do that as John Colton, Laura. I'm not going to be Prince James Wyndham. That's not who I am, not after all these years. I'm also going to have Jeremiah's birth certificate changed and his name will be Jeremiah Wyndham Colton.''

''Well, that's...nice,'' Laura said, tears brimming her eyes. ''You certainly have found all the answers you were seeking, haven't you? Yes, you have. I'm...I'm happy for you, John, I truly am. So! You're all set. Isn't that something? I'm very tired and I'm off to bed. Thank you for sharing your lovely news with me and—''

John cut off Laura's tear-filled babble by sliding his hand from the back of the sofa to the nape of her neck and capturing her lips with his.

Laura's eyes widened in shock, then in the next breathless moment her lashes drifted down as she savored the taste of John and the heated passion that suffused her.

John broke the kiss. Laura blinked and drew a trembling breath.

''There's just one more thing,'' John said, close to her lips. ''At long last I know what I need to be truly at peace, truly happy. I'm free to live and free...to love." He gazed into her eyes for a long moment. "Oh, Laura, I love you so much."

"What?" she whispered.

"I love you, Laura Bishop, with every breath in my body. We can have it all, *we can,* if you'll agree to be my wife, my partner in life, my soul mate until death parts us. Will you marry me? Live with me on the island of Wynborough as Laura Bishop Colton, help me raise *our* son, Jeremiah Wyndham Colton, and have a bunch more Colton babies with me?"

Emotions closed John's throat for a moment and he paused.

"Will you, Laura?" he said, his voice gritty. "Please?"

"Oh, dear heaven," she whispered, tears spilling onto her cheeks. "Oh...John...yes! I love you with all my heart, and I love Jeremiah...our son."

"Thank God," he said, his shoulders slumping. "I was so afraid that I was going to blow it, not say it right, mess up our entire future, because I'm lousy at putting my feelings into words. I haven't had much practice at it...you know what I mean? And I—"

This time it was *Laura* who silenced *John's* chatter with a kiss.

A kiss that sealed their commitment to a future together.

A kiss that marked the end of confusion and heartache.

A kiss that chased the chill of loneliness into

oblivion and replaced it with comforting warmth, which was quickly fanned into heated desire that consumed them.

John tore his mouth from Laura's and drew a rough breath.

"Wait." He brushed his lips over Laura's. "Not for long, believe me, because I'm going up in flames here, but...wait."

"Hmm?" Laura said dreamily.

John gripped both of her hands with his, and she blinked back to attention.

"Listen, okay?" John said. "After I talked to Phillip and things fell into place for me, there was one very...well, imperative piece still missing from that rosy picture."

"Oh?" Laura said.

John smiled at her warmly. "You. I was hanging on for dear life to the fact that you'd said you'd lost your heart to me. And I was hoping, praying that you hadn't managed to fall *out* of love with me."

"Never," Laura said, matching his smile.

"I had come within a breath of telling you how much I love you, Laura."

"The important discussion you wanted to have with me but didn't?"

"Yeah," John said, "that's the one. I pulled back because I believed I didn't have the right to express my feelings for you because I hadn't yet found inner peace and happiness. How could I begin to make *you* happy if I was floundering in a sea of confusion?"

"Oh, John."

"But once my future plans were set, I came looking for you," he went on. "Alex told me you were spending the day in Hope. I drove into town myself, not to find you, but to take care of a special errand."

"I thought I saw you," Laura said, "but I convinced myself it was just wishful thinking."

John chuckled. "I was skulking around, not wanting to bump into you for fear that I'd blurt out everything in front of the citizens of Hope." His smile faded. "Anyway, I found what I was looking for. If you don't like it, I'll return it for what you'd rather have, but..." He shrugged.

"The suspense is killing me," Laura said. "What are you talking about?"

John unsnapped the pocket on his Western shirt and removed a ring.

"Maybe you'd prefer a traditional diamond engagement ring," he said, "but I bought you an opal. Why? Ah, my Laura, because the colors of an opal reminded me of a rainbow. This ring represents my heartfelt love, and my determination to make your rainbow wish come true."

"Oh-h-h," Laura said, tears filling her eyes.

John frowned. "Could you translate that for me? Do you like the ring?"

"Yes, oh, yes," she said, sniffling.

John slipped the ring on Laura's finger and she gazed at it, the firelight causing the colors of the rainbow opal to sparkle.

"It's beautiful, John," she whispered. "Thank you."

John stood and drew Laura up into his arms.

"Let's go home," he said, "to our little cabin in the woods."

"Betty is there."

"She said she'd give me until midnight to convince you to marry me. I just made it. She'll be full of herself because she'll be the first to know our news."

He laughed softly.

"I have to warn you, though, Laura, that it won't come as a surprise to anyone. My whole family was aware of how we felt about each other. They were just waiting for us to figure everything out." He paused. "Let me rephrase that. They're *our* family."

John helped Laura on with her coat, then encircled her shoulders with one arm, nestling her close to his side.

They went out into the crisp night air to make their way to the cabin. Laura glanced up at the millions of stars twinkling in the black velvet sky.

And for one heart-stopping moment, she was certain, totally convinced, that she saw a glorious rainbow in the heavens.

Epilogue

It was a picture-perfect spring day on the island of Wynborough, as though Mother Nature had known that the special occasion deserved her finest effort.

Excitement crackled through the air on this, the day everyone had been eagerly awaiting; the celebration of the twentieth anniversary of the coronation of King Phillip Wyndham of Wynborough.

Royals, high-ranking officials and press corps from around the world had been arriving steadily during the past week to take part in the festivities.

Wyndham Castle where Queen Gabriella and King Phillip resided was bustling with activity and overflowing with guests.

John Colton strode down a long corridor in the royal home, Jeremiah perched on his shoulders. John returned smiles and nods of people he knew, as well as strangers gathered to honor his father.

He entered a large office, an instant smile lighting up his face as he saw the woman he'd come looking for.

"Hello, lovely wife," he said. "Jeremiah and I are here as you instructed to tell you it's time for all of us to change clothes, get spit-shined and pretty for the big doings." John paused. "Still glad you married me?"

Laura Bishop Colton laughed in delight where she stood behind a gleaming desk.

"Goodness," she said, "I must be having fun being married to you, John Colton, because I've lost all track of time."

"True," he said. "I'm a fun guy. We won't mention how busy we've been since our wedding. Hey, Jeremiah and I just walked over to look at the land we picked out to build our house on."

"Is it still there?" Laura said. "You two have made that trek every day for a week."

"Not only is the land still there, but some construction supplies have been delivered to our stretch of dirt. How about that?

"And how about you quit working for today, Ms. Social Secretary, so we can take part in the big shebang? You were the one who said I should haul you out of here on time."

"Yes, I'm coming right now," Laura said. "I've just been logging in the multitude of telegrams that have been arriving with messages of congratulations to Gabriella and Phillip. Oh, this is such an exciting day and... What's this?''

''What's what?'' John said as Jeremiah beat a rhythm on the top of his father's head.

''That's strange,'' Laura said. ''There's an envelope here among the Wyndham correspondence that is addressed to Victor Thorton, the Grand Duke of Thortonburg.''

John shrugged. ''Bring it along. I saw Victor Thorton a few minutes ago. We'll bump into him again at some point, and you can give him his letter. Hey, Jeremiah, quit pulling my hair. Laura, our son is demolishing me here. Let's go.''

''We're off,'' Laura said, coming from behind the desk with the envelope in question. ''Jeremiah, be nice to your daddy. After all, you're getting a marvelous view of everything from way up there.''

''Dada,'' Jeremiah said merrily, pulling John's hair again.

''Ow,'' John said. ''Cut it out.''

''Out. Out. Out,'' the baby yelled.

''Which is what is going to happen to my hair if you don't stop it,'' John said.

The trio left the office to go to their suite of rooms in the palace where they were living until their own home could be built.

As they reached the stairs leading to the private quarters on the upper floor, Laura saw Victor Thorton approaching them.

''Perfect,'' she said as he drew closer. ''You must be a mind reader, Your Grace.''

The tall, silver-haired man in his early sixties stopped, a smile breaking across his face as he wiggled Jeremiah's foot.

"Whose mind have I read, my dear Princess?" he said.

"Mine. This letter came for you, most likely from someone who knew you'd be in attendance at the celebration."

The Grand Duke accepted the envelope, slipped open the flap, then pulled free a piece of paper. Another enclosure fluttered to the floor and Laura retrieved it.

As the Grand Duke read the note, the color drained from his face.

"No, this is impossible." He looked at Laura, a stricken expression on his face. "What dropped onto the floor?"

"This picture of a pretty young woman," she said, handing it to him. "What's wrong?"

The Grand Duke's hand trembled as he stared at the photograph Laura had given him.

"It's true," he said. "There's no denying it, but I didn't know until this very moment." He shook his head, unable to speak as he was overcome with emotion.

"Know...what?" John said, frowning. "Who is that woman in the picture?"

"My daughter," Victor said. "This child I didn't even know I had has been kidnapped."

*   *   *   *   *

Turn the page for a sneak preview of

A ROYAL MASQUERADE

*by beloved author
Arlene James,*

*on sale in
Silhouette Romance
in March 2000.*

**As ROYALLY WED *continues,*
*a skeleton in the Thortons' closet
rears its head!***

"To the Grand Duke of Thortonburg. I have your daughter. Before you throw her life away as you did that of her mother, Maribelle, take a good look at the enclosed photograph. No doubt you'll agree that the family resemblance is pronounced. Add to this the existence of a raspberry birthmark in the shape of a teardrop and identification is a certainty."

Prince Roland Thorton traded looks with his brother, Prince Raphael. The birthmark was a closely guarded family secret, a hedge against impostors, a secret held by generations of Thortons—until now. Royal bodyguard Lance Grayson went on reading.

"The life of an innocent young woman may mean nothing to you, but have no doubt that the world will know your dirty secrets if you fail to follow my future instructions. Do nothing until then."

And it was signed, "The Justicier."

Victor Thorton, the Grand Duke of Thortonburg, handed over the photograph. Rafe stepped close to Roland and lifted the small, camera-developed snapshot. The resemblance was unmistakable. Dark hair, blue eyes, patrician features in an oval face. She was smiling, the photo obviously having been taken in an unguarded moment. Roland felt his heart lurch. His sister. A surge of fierce protectiveness surprised him.

"She looks to be about my age," he said.

"A year older, I would expect," Victor confirmed. He turned to his wife defensively. "It happened over twenty-seven years ago. We married for duty, Sara, but love came later, didn't it?"

She nodded, dabbing at the corners of her eyes with a linen handkerchief that had appeared from somewhere. For a long moment, Sara Thorton said nothing, merely stared sadly at her husband, but then she lifted her hand to her face and skimmed away her tears. "Roland came after our reconciliation. You've given me two wonderful sons, one out of duty and one out of love. But I always wanted a daughter, and you gave her to another woman."

Victor pursed his lips, obviously fighting his own

emotions. "I didn't want to hurt you," he said finally. "I wanted to spare you this knowledge. I wanted to spare us both this moment. I never knew about the child, but if she's mine, and it seems that she is, I must find her."

"It could be an elaborate hoax," Grayson pointed out. "The girl may not be a Thorton at all. We have to find out what has become of this Maribelle and whether or not she even has a daughter."

Roland glanced down at the photo that he had taken from his brother's hand. His gut told him this was no hoax, but they had to be sure. Meanwhile, they had to consider what to do next. The trouble was that his own mind was whirling.

"Could I see that, please, Roland."

The sound of his mother's voice brought his gaze up from the face on the photo.

"She's very beautiful," the Grand Duchess said at last, "and every inch a Thorton." She looked up at the assembled group and asked, "Who could do this, kidnap an innocent young woman and hold her for ransom?"

The atmosphere in the room changed somehow, coalesced with a fresh, strong sense of purpose. They were banded together as a family in that moment, united in support of their own, as they never had been before. Roland felt an overwhelming sense of pride.

"Charles Montague." Victor turned his head to impale his youngest son with a sharp gaze. "The shipping contract."

Roland nodded, thinking it through. "It could be that, not knowing the matter is already resolved, Charles Montague means to force you to withdraw your bid. But why? He's never gone to such lengths before."

"Given Raphael's marriage to Princess Elizabeth of Wynborough, Montague might have assumed that he needed an upper hand in the negotiations. He could have discovered the girl accidentally and had her kidnapped in an effort to force us to back out of negotiations. It must be Montague!" Victor exclaimed.

Suddenly Roland knew exactly who could accomplish the task of investigating the Montagues. He had played his role in the Thortonburg ruling family in relative obscurity. Never the heir, he was ignored by most in upper echelons in government. He'd made sure to keep himself out of the papers and off the news. Moreover, the enmity between the Montagues and the Thortons had insured that a certain distance was kept by the families.

"We need someone inside Roxbury," Roland said, "someone who can get close to the Montagues, someone utterly trustworthy who knows what he's about and can make himself invisible."

Victor looked at Roland in surprise. "Who?"

Roland, coldly purposeful, kept his smile tight and said, "Me."

Silhouette Romance is
proud to announce the
exciting continuation of

*This time, Thorton royal
family secrets are exposed!*

A Royal Masquerade
by Arlene James (#1432)
On sale March 2000

A Royal Marriage
by Cara Colter (#1440)
On sale April 2000

A Royal Mission
by Elizabeth August (#1446)
On sale May 2000

Available at your favorite retail outlet.

®
™

Where love comes alive ™

Visit us at www.romance.net

SSERW2

Looking For More Romance?

Visit Romance.net

Look us up on-line at: http://www.romance.net

Check in daily for these and other exciting features:

Hot off the press

View all current titles, and purchase them on-line.

What do the stars have in store for you?

Horoscope

Hot deals

Exclusive offers available only at Romance.net

Plus, don't miss our interactive quizzes, contests and bonus gifts.

PWEB

Celebrate the joy of bringing a baby into the world—
and the power of passionate love—with

A Bouquet of Babies

An anthology containing three delightful stories
from three beloved authors!

THE WAY HOME

The classic tale from *New York Times* bestselling author

LINDA HOWARD

FAMILY BY FATE

A brand-new Maternity Row story by

PAULA DETMER RIGGS

BABY ON HER DOORSTEP

A brand-new Twins on the Doorstep story by

STELLA BAGWELL

Available in April 2000, at your favorite retail outlet.

Silhouette®

Where love comes alive™

MONTANA MAVERICKS
Big Sky Brides

Legendary love comes to Whitehorn, Montana,
once more as beloved authors

Christine Rimmer, Jennifer Greene and Cheryl St.John

present three brand-new stories in this exciting anthology!

Meet the Brennan women:
SUZANNA, DIANA and ISABELLE

Strong-willed beauties who find unexpected
love in these irresistible marriage of
covnenience stories.

Don't miss
MONTANA MAVERICKS: BIG SKY BRIDES
On sale in February 2000,
only from Silhouette Books!

Available at your favorite retail outlet.

Visit us at www.romance.net   PSMMBSB

PAMELA TOTH
DIANA WHITNEY
ALLISON LEIGH
LAURIE PAIGE
bring you four heartwarming stories
in the brand-new series

So Many Babies

At the Buttonwood Baby Clinic,
babies and romance abound!

♥♥♥♥♥♥♥♥♥

On sale January 2000: **THE BABY LEGACY**
by Pamela Toth

On sale February 2000: **WHO'S THAT BABY?**
by Diana Whitney

On sale March 2000: **MILLIONAIRE'S INSTANT BABY**
by Allison Leigh

On sale April 2000: **MAKE WAY FOR BABIES!**
by Laurie Paige

***Only from Silhouette* SPECIAL EDITION**
Available at your favorite retail outlet.

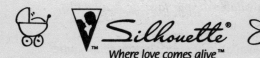 *Silhouette®*
Where love comes alive™

Silhouette Special Edition brings you

AND BABY MAKES THREE
The Delacourts of Texas

by SHERRYL WOODS

*Come join the Delacourt family as they all find love—
and parenthood—in the most unexpected ways!*

On sale December 1999:
THE COWBOY AND THE NEW YEAR'S BABY (SE#1291)
During one of the worst blizzards in Texas history, a
stranded Trish Delacourt was about to give birth! Luckily,
sexy Hardy Jones rushed to the rescue. Could the no-strings
bachelor and the new mom turn a precious New Year's
miracle into a labor of *love?*

On sale March 2000:
DYLAN AND THE BABY DOCTOR (SE#1309)
Private detective Dylan Delacourt had closed off part of
his heart and wasn't prepared for what Kelsey James stirred
up when she called on him to locate her missing son.

And don't miss Jeb Delacourt's story coming
to Special Edition in July 2000.

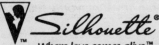

Silhouette ®
Where love comes alive ™

Available at your favorite retail outlet.

SILHOUETTE'S 20TH ANNIVERSARY CONTEST
OFFICIAL RULES
NO PURCHASE NECESSARY TO ENTER

1. To enter, follow directions published in the offer to which you are responding. Contest begins 1/1/00 and ends on 8/24/00 (the "Promotion Period"). Method of entry may vary. Mailed entries must be postmarked by 8/24/00, and received by 8/31/00.

2. During the Promotion Period, the Contest may be presented via the Internet. Entry via the Internet may be restricted to residents of certain geographic areas that are disclosed on the Web site. To enter via the Internet, if you are a resident of a geographic area in which Internet entry is permissible, follow the directions displayed on-line, including typing your essay of 100 words or fewer telling us "Where In The World Your Love Will Come Alive." On-line entries must be received by 11:59 p.m. Eastern Standard time on 8/24/00. Limit one e-mail entry per person, household and e-mail address per day, per presentation. If you are a resident of a geographic area in which entry via the Internet is permissible, you may, in lieu of submitting an entry on-line, enter by mail, by hand-printing your name, address, telephone number and contest number/name on an 8"x 11" plain piece of paper and telling us in 100 words or fewer "Where In The World Your Love Will Come Alive," and mailing via first-class mail to: Silhouette 20th Anniversary Contest, (in the U.S.) P.O. Box 9069, Buffalo, NY 14269-9069; (In Canada) P.O. Box 637, Fort Erie, Ontario, Canada L2A 5X3. Limit one 8"x 11" mailed entry per person, household and e-mail address per day. On-line and/or 8"x 11" mailed entries received from persons residing in geographic areas in which Internet entry is not permissible will be disqualified. No liability is assumed for lost, late, incomplete, inaccurate, nondelivered or misdirected mail, or misdirected e-mail, for technical, hardware or software failures of any kind, lost or unavailable network connection, or failed, incomplete, garbled or delayed computer transmission or any human error which may occur in the receipt or processing of the entries in the contest.

3. Essays will be judged by a panel of members of the Silhouette editorial and marketing staff based on the following criteria:

> Sincerity (believability, credibility)—50%
> Originality (freshness, creativity)—30%
> Aptness (appropriateness to contest ideas)—20%

Purchase or acceptance of a product offer does not improve your chances of winning. In the event of a tie, duplicate prizes will be awarded.

4. All entries become the property of Harlequin Enterprises Ltd., and will not be returned. Winner will be determined no later than 10/31/00 and will be notified by mail. Grand Prize winner will be required to sign and return Affidavit of Eligibility within 15 days of receipt of notification. Noncompliance within the time period may result in disqualification and an alternative winner may be selected. All municipal, provincial, federal, state and local laws and regulations apply. Contest open only to residents of the U.S. and Canada who are 18 years of age or older, and is void wherever prohibited by law. Internet entry is restricted solely to residents of those geographical areas in which Internet entry is permissible. Employees of Torstar Corp., their affiliates, agents and members of their immediate families are not eligible. Taxes on the prizes are the sole responsibility of winners. Entry and acceptance of any prize offered constitutes permission to use winner's name, photograph or other likeness for the purposes of advertising, trade and promotion on behalf of Torstar Corp. without further compensation to the winner, unless prohibited by law. Torstar Corp and D.L. Blair, Inc., their parents, affiliates and subsidiaries, are not responsible for errors in printing or electronic presentation of contest or entries. In the event of printing or other errors which may result in unintended prize values or duplication of prizes, all affected contest materials or entries shall be null and void. If for any reason the Internet portion of the contest is not capable of running as planned, including infection by computer virus, bugs, tampering, unauthorized intervention, fraud, technical failures, or any other causes beyond the control of Torstar Corp. which corrupt or affect the administration, secrecy, fairness, integrity or proper conduct of the contest, Torstar Corp. reserves the right, at its sole discretion, to disqualify any individual who tampers with the entry process and to cancel, terminate, modify or suspend the contest or the Internet portion thereof. In the event of a dispute regarding an on-line entry, the entry will be deemed submitted by the authorized holder of the e-mail account submitted at the time of entry. Authorized account holder is defined as the natural person who is assigned to an e-mail address by an Internet access provider, on-line service provider or other organization that is responsible for arranging e-mail address for the domain associated with the submitted e-mail address.

5. Prizes: Grand Prize—a $10,000 vacation to anywhere in the world. Travelers (at least one must be 18 years of age or older) or parent or guardian if one traveler is a minor, must sign and return a Release of Liability prior to departure. Travel must be completed by December 31, 2001, and is subject to space and accommodations availability. Two hundred (200) Second Prizes—a two-book limited edition autographed collector set from one of the Silhouette Anniversary authors: Nora Roberts, Diana Palmer, Linda Howard or Annette Broadrick (value $10.00 each set). All prizes are valued in U.S. dollars.

6. For a list of winners (available after 10/31/00), send a self-addressed, stamped envelope to: Harlequin Silhouette 20th Anniversary Winners, P.O. Box 4200, Blair, NE 68009-4200.

Contest sponsored by Torstar Corp., P.O. Box 9042, Buffalo, NY 14269-9042.

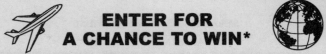

ENTER FOR
A CHANCE TO WIN*

Silhouette's 20th Anniversary Contest

Tell Us Where in the World
You Would Like *Your* Love To Come Alive...
And We'll Send the Lucky Winner There!

Silhouette wants to take you wherever
your happy ending can come true.

Here's how to enter: Tell us, in 100 words or less,
where you want to go to make your love come alive!

In addition to the grand prize, there will be 200
runner-up prizes, collector's-edition book sets
autographed by one of the Silhouette anniversary
authors: **Nora Roberts, Diana Palmer,
Linda Howard** or **Annette Broadrick**.

DON'T MISS YOUR CHANCE TO WIN!
ENTER NOW! No Purchase Necessary

Silhouette®
Where love comes alive™

Name:

Address:

City: State/Province:

Zip/Postal Code:

Mail to Harlequin Books: **In the U.S.**: P.O. Box 9069, Buffalo, NY
14269-9069; **In Canada**: P.O. Box 637, Fort Erie, Ontario, L4A 5X3

*No purchase necessary—for contest details send a self-addressed stamped envelope to:
Silhouette's 20th Anniversary Contest, P.O. Box 9069, Buffalo, NY, 14269-9069 (include
contest name on self-addressed envelope). Residents of Washington and Vermont may
omit postage. Open to Cdn. (excluding Quebec) and U.S. residents who are 18 or over.
Void where prohibited. Contest ends August 31, 2000.

PS20CON_R